DON'T PUSH ME

DON'T PUSH ME

MICHAEL HARTWIG

Contents

Special Thanks

Special thanks go to François Kocher - friend, historian, and ski enthusiast. François grew up skiing in Grindelwald and the Jungfrau region. He has an encyclopedic knowledge of the slopes and lifts and their evolution over the years. He offered important insights, language edits, creative ideas, and critical historical perspectives throughout the writing process. He has a keen eye for detail and was generous in sharing information about this beautiful part of Switzerland. Needless to say, any inaccuracies are the result of creative license. It was during a visit several years ago to see him and his wife, Kathy, that I first fell in love with winter in the Bernese Oberland. I felt a deep and instant connection to the place - one that has led me back each winter to ski and one that led to the discovery of the fascinating history surrounding World War 1 and the early days of British skiing in Mürren. Thanks François!

Work of Fiction

This is a work of fiction. Names, characters, places and incidents either are products of the author's imagination or are used fictitiously. Any resemblance to actual events or locales or persons, living or dead, is entirely coincidental.

Cover Art

Cover by author; image licensed from Shutterstock.

1

Chapter One – The Gasthof Traumblick

Mürren Winter 2007

Elliott stepped off the train, dragging skis, boots, and suitcase through a fresh blanket of snow that covered the rustic platform. Flurries filled the air, with a mix of sun and clouds hovering overhead. He breathed in the fresh mountain air and smiled, glad he had finally arrived. A frenetic crowd of tourists disembarked, balancing luggage, ski equipment, and restless children.

He glanced at a small map he pulled from his pocket, checking directions to the Gasthof Traumblick, his home for the next two weeks. It looked like it was a short walk from the station - about 10 minutes. He walked up the slight incline of the main road, grateful his boots gripped the surface of the slippery path. Rowdy kids threw snowballs and pushed each other as parents yelled instructions about the trek forward. Gratefully, most headed into the larger hotels at the center of town. Elliott continued to the other side of the village, where things were noticeably calmer.

Mürren was the idyllic Alpine village every English skier dreamed of – a car free town perched high in the Bernese Oberland. It was known for its dramatic views of the Lauterbrunnen Valley with the glacier studded peaks of the Eiger, Mönch, and Jungfrau towering in the distance. The town looked as if it were about to slide off a two-thousand-foot cliff with tall pine trees clinging tenaciously to a snow-covered rocky bluff. Towering summits surrounded the plateau on which the town sat, including the famous Schilthorn, where James Bond defied gravity, skiing through forests to the valley floor.

From time to time, skiers skidded to a stop just at the edge of the pedestrian road, having navigated charming trails that began in the snowfields at higher altitudes and ended in the hamlet of wooden ski chalets and inns. Elliott couldn't help noticing the delight on skiers' faces as they removed goggles and glanced up at what they had traversed. He was eager to join them.

The Gasthof Traumblick had an enviable setting with unobstructed views of the surrounding landscape. A large expanse of pristine snow stretched from the side of the building toward the edge of the precipice. Elliott wondered if people ever got too close to the edge. He felt his heart race just thinking about it.

A path from the main road to the entrance of the inn had been cleared. The snowbanks were several feet high, promising great conditions on the pistes. Elliott pushed open the antique wooden door and heard a bell announce his arrival. He dragged his equipment and luggage into the cozy foyer, stomped snow off his boots, and waited for someone to appear at the check-in counter.

A man stepped out from a room behind the counter and said, "*Guten Tag.*"

Elliott responded in his modest German, "*Hallo. Mein Name ist Elliott. Elliott Williams.*"

"Ah, yes. Mr. Williams. Welcome. I'm Max. How was your journey?" the man replied in perfect English.

"Long," Elliott replied, reviewing in his head the many means of transport it took to arrive at his destination – the flight from London, the train from the Zurich airport to Interlaken, another train to Lauterbrunnen, a cable car to Grütschalp, and the final train to Mürren.

"It's part of the charm — our remoteness!"

"Hmm," Elliott murmured. The scenery was breathtaking, and he was eager to ski the world-famous slopes, but he had a foreboding sense that perhaps Mürren was too isolated for his tastes.

"Your passport?" Max asked as he slid a registration form toward Elliott to complete.

Elliott reached into his coat pocket and pulled out his documents, glancing into Max's eyes as he handed them over. They were hazel, expressive, and intense. Max had a distinguished receding hairline with salt and pepper wavy hair – more pepper than salt. He had a large sexy nose and a pronounced jaw that was lined with a closely trimmed dark beard. Elliott took a deep breath. The name of the hotel seemed to denote more than just the dreamy views of the mountains.

"You're alone?" Max asked, glancing around the foyer as if expecting a companion or children.

"Yes. Did you think there would be more?"

"Well, it's just that you booked one of our family suites. But it's fine."

"It looked like a splendid room online. The photos showed it had wonderful views and a comfortable sitting area."

"Yes. I'm sure you will enjoy it. Here's the key. It's on the third floor, facing the valley. Dinner is at seven. If there's anything you need, don't hesitate to let us know. We are a small, family-run inn, and we want to make our guests feel at home."

"*Danke schön*," Elliott replied. He left his skis in the ski closet on the first floor and carried his luggage and boot bag up the steep wooden stairs to the third floor.

He opened the door and took a deep breath. The room was impressive, with unparalleled views of the nearby peaks. Bright light filled the wood paneled apartment. There was a cozy sitting area with a sofa, coffee table, and lamp. The bed was large, with a carved wooden headboard and decorative Swiss blankets and pillows covering the mattress. The updated and stylish bathroom had a large soaking tub.

Elliott unpacked, hanging ski clothes, pants, and sweaters in an antique wooden armoire. He placed other items in the drawer of a chest. He sat down in a comfortable chair near the window and began to identify landmarks. The train from Kleine Scheidegg was making its way toward Wengen, a charming ski town just across the valley from Mürren. Late day, purplish shadows from the soaring peaks spread quickly over the lower terrain. The iconic Jungfrau towered above the other summits, reflecting the late afternoon golden sunlight.

As he aged, Elliott became more cognizant of the power of mountains. Their solidity made him feel safe, grounded, strong. Their height drew his gaze upward. When dressed in clouds or snow, they were mysterious, concealing spirits who retreated out of view. The Jungfrau range stood just outside his window; a massive ensemble of peaks that seemed almost close enough to touch. The frenetic pace of life and the troubles of home seemed trivial compared to the scene before him. Even the wintery Alps were sunny and warm compared to the damp, dreary Yorkshire countryside.

Hungry from the long day of travel, Elliott made his way downstairs to the parlor. Orange light from crackling logs in the stone fireplace filled the cozy room. Families had gathered before dinner to play board games and sip hot chocolate. Elliott found an out-of-the-way comfortable chair where he sat and thumbed through a local tourist magazine. It surprised him that most of the clientele were English and Dutch, except for one Swiss family and a German one. They were a well-heeled crowd, although not the rich-and-famous kind. These were affluent families able to afford a couple of weeks in the Alps, but not at the chic resorts. He surmised it must have been school vacation week, given the large number of children.

He was the only single person in the room and hoped there might be more at dinner. Feeling a slight pinch in his chest, he contemplated the idea of being trapped with a bunch of families in the Alps. Several of the men were handsome, particularly a dark-haired English man with two adorable kids. He and his wife sat close to each other on a sofa, watching their kids play cards. They sipped brandy. The woman was beautiful with brunette hair, thick eyebrows, and caramel complexion. He surmised she might have been Italian or French. The man nodded warmly at Elliott.

The family from Germany dominated the room. Their kids were playful, talkative, and athletic. The wife was short but pleasant, even pretty in her own way. The husband was imposing with a broad muscular chest, large bulging thighs, and a thick playful head of hair. He was tall and had a deep, thunderous voice. He spoke English well, making small friendly talk with the English families nearby.

A woman came out into the parlor and announced that dinner was ready. The kids leaped up from their games and ran into the dining room. Parents followed. Everyone seemed to have assigned tables.

The woman approached Elliott and introduced herself. "I'm Sofia, one of the owners. You met Max earlier. Welcome. Is everything to your satisfaction in your room?"

"It's perfect. What a beautiful inn. I love the woodwork and comfortable furniture and artistic touches here and there."

"Thank you. It's a labor of love." Sofia had a warm smile. She looked like she was in her late forties. She had shiny blonde hair and golden skin. Gesturing to Elliot, she said, "Let me show you to your table."

They walked into the spacious dining room. Antique wood beams supported the ceiling. Along one wall, there was a line of tables separated by carved wooden dividers and lit by antique brass lamps. A large window faced the Jungfrau mountains where several free-standing tables were set. The rest of the room had a variety of table settings, including one small table off to itself. "That's your table. I hope it will be quiet," she said, glancing around the room filled with kids.

Elliott thanked her and took his place. A small team of servers circulated through the space, filling bowls with a savory soup and asking for drink orders. Elliott ordered some Swiss wine.

Despite the carpeting that would have softened the noise, the room was raucous, with kids yelling at each other and parents admonishing them as they tried unsuccessfully to eat dinner and enjoy their vacation. Elliott observed from a distance, increasingly concerned that he had chosen the wrong hotel for his ski trip.

Max, who was prepping plates, observed him from behind a side door and shook his head, nervous his guest would soon begin to make complaints. Max found Elliott's presence intriguing and a bit unnerving. Innkeeping was a curious business. One invited people into one's home, made them comfortable, fed them, and invited them to relax and enjoy themselves. It was always a delicate balance between familiarity and formality, between warmth and business.

Max knew how to manage married couples; how to de-escalate tensions with humor and carry on conversations about inane superficial topics. No one had the time or energy after a day on the slopes with their kids to ask Max personal questions or start deeper conversations about politics, philosophy, or culture. Sure, with married couples, there was always one, or both, who fantasized about escaping the quagmire of parenting responsibilities and relentless crises. They flirted with Max, and he enjoyed the attention, but nothing serious ever unfolded.

Max couldn't remember the last time they had a single guest who wasn't part of a larger booking of a family or group of friends. He wondered if Elliott had an agenda. How did he end up at the Traumblick? Would Elliott disturb Max's carefully constructed world and life, engaging him in uncomfortable conversation or personal questions?

Max felt himself tense up. Sofia walked by and could see the concern on his face. "What's wrong?" she asked.

"I don't know. This new guest. Does he seem odd to you?"

She glanced through the door and peered at Elliott. She replied, "He seems like a nice man. Speaks German. Is well dressed."

"Don't you find it a bit odd – a single man at our inn?"

Sofia hesitated. She, too, wondered how he ended up at their inn, but Mürren was a quiet and out-of-the-way place that didn't usually attract shifty types. She said, "He'll be fine. He likes to ski."

"But the noise. He's going to get annoyed."

"He's on the third floor. It's quiet."

Max shook his head. He had an unsettled foreboding. He continued to prep plates, and Sofia returned to her chores.

Over the course of the next half hour, Max scrutinized Elliott. He had a book open at his table. He sipped his wine and consumed the soup while remaining focused on what he was reading. He glanced up from time to time, startled by a child's scream or a kid running between the tables. Elliott ordered a second half-liter of wine; not a good sign, Max thought.

Sofia glanced from around the door, too. She noticed Elliott on his cell phone. She feared he might be reporting his bad luck at booking the Traumblick to a friend back home.

"Marni," Elliott said excitedly as the woman on the other end of the line answered. "I'm here. It's dreadful. A dining room filled with kids and their parents."

"So, you arrived without problems?"

"Yes, but this is a mistake. It's school vacation week, and I'm at an Alpine resort where half of the suburbs of London have come to get away - all with children."

"Any cute or handsome daddies?"

"Marni! I'm serious. This has catastrophe written all over it."

"I'm serious, too. Take a more optimistic view of things. Look for opportunities, even in unpleasant situations. They're always there. Who knows what hot daddy is looking for a reason to come out; to admit he married the wrong sex and needs someone to guide him in a new direction."

"I'm not here to save anyone. I'm here to relax, ski, and find out more about the connections between my grandfather and Mürren."

Despite his protests, Elliott took another look around the room. The same two men caught his attention – the handsome, dark-haired English guy and the imposing German jock.

"I told you that you should have booked in Verbier or Zermatt. I don't even know where Mürren is. It's got to be boring."

"The scenery is breathtaking – there just don't seem to be any single men around."

"Go out to a club. You'll meet people. You always do."

"I am not sure there are clubs in this town."

"Ask the innkeepers."

At that moment, Max leaned his head around the kitchen door. Elliott caught his attention and nodded. Max felt compelled to approach Elliott and ask how he was doing, dreading his response.

Elliott told Marni, "Got to go. The innkeeper is approaching."

"*Ciao*," she said.

"Mr. Williams, how are things?" Max asked as he stood at the edge of the small wooden table.

"My room is very nice, and the food is delicious. It's a little loud, though. That's all," he said as he looked around the room.

Max followed Elliott's regard, scanning the dining room. "Hmm," he murmured. "It is school winter vacation. Lots of families." He glanced back at Elliott with an apologetic face, scrutinizing his new guest. He seemed unusually fussy and wore a starched white shirt under an alpine sweater. The book on the table was perfectly aligned with the grain of the tabletop, and a bookmark had been carefully positioned between pages and just a centimeter above the edge of the paper. Elliott's knife and fork were evenly spaced on either side of the plate, and Elliott kept rearranging the small vase and candle. Max noticed the title of the book – *The Challenges of the European Central Bank*.

"Looks like a riveting read," Max said playfully.

Elliott didn't respond, sensing Max was making light of his choice for vacation reading.

Max picked up on Elliott's prickliness and changed the subject, asking, "Are you looking forward to skiing? Tomorrow promises to be a great day. Anything we can do to assist you?"

"I think I'm fine. I already have lift tickets. Any suggestions for good areas to ski?"

"If tomorrow is a warmup day, you might try Winteregg or Schiltgrat. They are both nice areas with good runs – nothing too challenging."

Elliott nodded. He looked distracted. He fussed nervously with his fork, glancing toward the kitchen as if expecting the main course to arrive. Max interpreted Elliott's behavior as one of a pretentious businessman used to more indulging service. His and Sofia's inn was small and catered to a casual and undemanding crowd.

"Thanks. Do you ski?" Elliott asked Max, looking up. Max looked nervous, his eyes darting back and forth at all the activity in the room. Elliott couldn't tell if it was a look of consternation or one of inadequacy, someone overwhelmed by the responsibilities of running a hotel and keeping everyone happy, even the single fussy guy.

Max nodded. "Yes. But with all the work here, I don't get out too often."

Elliott hoped to get more of a reading of Max, catch a glance, measure the intensity in his eyes. He had already tried to draw the attention of the handsome daddies in the room with no success. Perhaps the innkeeper had a roving eye.

Max continued to glance around the room, not at Elliott. As Max looked away, Elliott took a closer look at Max's physique – his slim waist, muscular legs, and firm buttocks. "Hmm. Nice," he murmured to himself.

Max turned around and peered at Elliott, taking another reading himself. Elliott had haunting eyes – brown and deeply set. He was one of those dark English types, with black wavy hair that glistened in the overhead light. He had a slender face with a forceful nose, a broad forehead, and delicious lips. Berating himself for studying his new guest's appearance, Max hoped Elliott couldn't detect his curiosity.

"It must be an occupational hazard – working in a beautiful ski village with little time to enjoy the slopes."

Max nodded. He was tempted to say, "Yes. We have to cater to all of you affluent businessmen who have the resources to get away," but he checked himself. He often resented his guests, although as he watched those with children, he realized the parents had a tough life and he was glad he could make their lives more enjoyable. Scrutinizing Elliott, he didn't feel the same compassion. He said matter-of-factly, "It's a good life." Then he let his guard down and said, "At least I don't have to go into the office every day."

Elliott felt the sting of Max's comment and reached for his glass of wine. He took a sip and said, "Well, you have a nice place here."

It was clearly a dismissal kind of remark. Max took the cue and excused himself. Elliott opened his book and continued to read.

The main course arrived shortly thereafter. It was a thin, breaded schnitzel with fries and red cabbage. The veal was delicate and savory, and the breaded coating had a unique but pleasing spice added. Elliott devoured the meal, having only snacked on the train ride up. For dessert, the server brought chocolate pudding and a cup of coffee.

Max made another round through the room, and Elliott raised his hand. Max approached, as if he had been summoned. "Mr. Williams? Can I be of service?"

"I just wanted to say that the food is amazing! Are you the cook?"

"Sofia and I share responsibilities in that area. When we are full, like now, we have a local woman who helps, too."

"Well, compliments!"

"Thank you." Max nodded and excused himself.

Elliott reached for his glass of wine and took a sip. He pulled some postcards and photos from inside the back of his book. When his mother passed the year before, he cleaned out the attic of their home. He found several boxes of memorabilia associated with his grandfather, Clive Williams. There were several old, yellow photos of soldiers in the Alps, some of them on skis. He knew his grandfather had served in the First World War and had learned that he was a prisoner in Switzerland. There were several postcards dated from the 1920s and later, several that included the return address of the Gasthof Traumblick.

His friend Marni had encouraged him to take some time, get away, meet people. During the final years of Elliott's mom's life, he had taken care of her and put his life on a back burner. "You're not getting any younger," his friend chastised him. "If you're going to meet someone, you need to get on with it."

Elliott had married when he was twenty-five, but he divorced ten years later. His wife, Milly, said he was cold, unaffectionate, and needed to deal with his sexual orientation. The shock of their rupture forced him to take an inventory of his life. He came out and began to date men, but he put his sexual exploits on hold when his father died and his mother became ill.

He looked up and scanned the room. "How pathetic," he whispered to himself. "You finally have the courage to take time off from work and start putting yourself out there and you end up at ski kindergarten."

2

Chapter Two – Grandpa Clive

Grindelwald Winter 1962

Elliott sat on the seat next to his grandfather, his legs dangling under him. He had new ski boots and kept admiring them in the bright sunshine streaming through the train windows. The cog train strained as it climbed the steep incline.

Elliott loved the passing scenery – the cavernous banks of snow through which the train traversed, groves of fir trees burdened with fresh snow glistening in the sun, wooden barns closed for the winter, their eaves sheltering stacks of firewood, and the ubiquitous bluish gray peaks towering overhead, studded with glaciers.

Elliott glanced around the carriage at the formidable bodies crowded around him. A group of teenagers had jumped on board at the Grund train station. Many wore the newest ski fashion – form-fitting stretch pants and thick, red ski sweaters. They stood proudly holding their long skis; their eyes hidden behind dark sunglasses.

Since it was Elliott's 10th birthday, his grandfather had offered to take him to the Alps for a ski vacation and buy him new equipment. Elliott's father, Henry, and his mother, Emma, had little interest in skiing. They considered such things extravagant and overly indulgent. Henry had a difficult time saying no to his father's generous offer to take his son on a trip, for which Elliott was grateful.

It was Elliott's first trip without his parents. He felt like an adult. He had his own plane ticket, carried his own luggage, and had a hotel room connected to his grandfather's. Of course, his grandfather was with him all the time. In the evening, they gathered for dinner in the hotel dining room and played cards afterwards near a fireplace in the hotel parlor.

Elliott looked up at Clive, now 67. Although he was one of the older people on the train, Elliott thought he might be the coolest passenger in the crowd. He wore dark stretch ski pants and a blue ski jacket. Even compared to the teens, his grandfather seemed in exceptional shape. He had broad shoulders, a robust chest, muscular legs, and a commanding height at six feet. He had stashed his new pair of Austrian skis by the train door, and he had new boots to match.

A couple of the teenagers giggled, whispering to one another and glancing in Clive's direction. One of them made a remark and Clive, in German, made an off-handed comment saying, "How many of you sissies will be skiing when you are my age?" He cocked his head, placed his dark glasses on his nose, and glanced off as if indifferent to them. Elliott grinned, grasping the bravura of his grandfather even if he didn't understand the language.

"Are you ready for a fun day on the slopes?" Clive asked Elliott. "Shall we go to the top of the Lauberhorn first?"

Elliott nodded excitedly. He had studied the ski map the night before. He knew that required taking a long T-bar up a steep mountain. It required stamina to reach the top, but the rewards were amazing, with vast cruising runs back to Kleine Scheidegg.

"Maybe later we can ski to Wengen and have lunch?" Clive added.

The teenagers pretended indifference to Clive's and Elliott's conversation, unable to comprehend their English. Elliott observed them carefully, trying to decipher their gestures and posture. They were aloof and cocky, but Elliott detected an underlying insecurity, the need for admiration and attention. He, too, wanted attention, rocking his new boots in front of him. One of the guys noticed and winked at him. Instinctively, Elliott broke out in a smile, but he knew he needed to conceal it; act as if it didn't matter to him. He peered up at his grandfather, who seemed particularly skilled at attracting attention and feigning indifference. At the moment, Elliott didn't fully appreciate the fact that he was taking more than ski lessons from his handsome grandfather.

The train pulled into Kleine Scheidegg, a hamlet of hotels and restaurants where trails and lifts serviced breathtaking ski terrain. People leaped out onto the platform, dragging skis and poles to the surrounding lifts and trails. It was a chaotic but thrilling moment – a sea of tan, beautiful, stylish, and fun-loving people beginning their day on the slopes.

"Follow me," Clive said to Elliott, leading him through the throng to a path that led to the Lauberhorn lift. "Now, fasten your skis." Elliott leaned over, stepped onto the bindings, and secured them. They were the new type of bindings that had a swivel release on the front toe and a clip for the heel. Clive stepped into his and fastened the cable as well. They walked herring bone style up a slight incline to the bottom of the lift. Elliott noticed the teens were still getting ready farther down the hill. He was proud of his clever and athletic grandfather.

The ride up the mountain was challenging - maintaining balance on the skis and staying in the track formed under the lift. At the top, they released the lift pole and slid to the side, where they adjusted boots and secured clothing. Elliott took a deep breath. The north face of the famous Eiger mountain loomed overhead, casting blue shadows on the ski terrain below. Elliott skied mostly in Scotland or at small family-oriented resorts in Austria. His grandfather once orchestrated a family trip to Grindelwald, but Elliott's father hated every minute, and they never returned.

During that trip, Elliott fell in love with the scenery, particularly the majestic peaks of the Wetterhorn, the Eiger, the Mönch, and the Jungfrau. From almost every run, there were breathtaking views of some of the most beautiful mountains in the Alps. It was hard not to stop and just stare at the panorama.

He sensed his grandfather loved the area as well. It was practically the only place he would ski, and Elliott noticed the satisfied smile on his grandfather's face as he surveyed the horizon and let the sun warm his face.

"Ready?" Grandpa Clive asked.

Elliott nodded. They pushed off. Elliott's grandfather was an expert skier. He made graceful and well-controlled turns on the soft fresh powder covering the trail. Elliott followed, mimicking his moves as best he could. He was still perfecting the stem christie turn, one that began with a wedge but followed with the sliding of the uphill ski closer to the downhill one.

Although there were some excellent skiers on the slopes, there were plenty of beginners. They made jerky turns, snowplowed to slow down, and often lost control, barreling down the steep runs.

"Keep the front of your chest facing downhill," his grandfather yelled as he stood on the side of the trail observing. "Point your poles where you want to turn," he added.

Several of the teens they had seen on the train raced past them, clearly out of control. Several crashed into a large snowbank at the edge of the trail. Elliott watched his grandfather push off and make elegant and fluid turns as he skied past them. Elliott followed, having a difficult time not staring at the young men brushing snow off their sweaters and sunglasses. He chuckled as he watched his grandfather continue down the run to Kleine Scheidegg. Elliott followed in his tracks, even artfully navigating a few snow bumps or moguls that had formed on the piste.

"That was splendid," Clive remarked as his grandson skied up to him and tossed some powder as he skidded to a stop. "You're becoming quite the skier," Clive said proudly of Elliott, patting him warmly on his shoulder. "Another run?"

Elliott nodded. They skied to the lift, grabbed a pole, and headed up the mountain again.

"So why doesn't dad like it here?" Elliott asked as the lift pulled them up the mountain.

"Hmm," Clive began. He realized it had a lot to do with himself, with how hard and demanding he was toward his son. Henry didn't like the cold and he didn't like the cumbersome ski equipment. But, most of all, his son was jealous. Clive couldn't hide his passion and obsession with this ski area. Henry never understood why his father talked about Grindelwald all the time, why he was frugal all year only to indulge in a ski holiday on the slopes. Clive answered as simply as possible, "Your dad doesn't like to ski that much."

Elliott nodded. The answer made sense. But Elliott was curious. "Why do you like it here so much?"

"Isn't it obvious? The scenery is magnificent, and the ski runs are fantastic."

Again, the straightforward answer made sense to a ten-year-old. Elliott wasn't ready for the more complicated and painful reason, Clive thought.

They soon arrived at the top of the Lauberhorn, and Clive led the way down a gentle slope toward the Lauberhorn race trail. It was the longest run in the men's downhill ski races, running from above Kleine Scheidegg down to Wengen, a car-free village just above the Lauterbrunnen Valley. At the top of the run, Clive asked, "We can take the easier run to town, but I think you might be ready for this one, the Lauberhorn Race. What do you think?"

Elliott looked down the mountain and noticed the considerable pitch of the piste. His heart raced in anticipation. He could feel his palms sweat and his feet get clammy. He took a deep breath and nodded timidly that he was ready to try it.

Clive said, "Most of the run is not that difficult, at least nothing more than what you are used to skiing already. The exception is the Hundschopf, a steep area where racers fly over a rocky drop. We'll ski around the rocks. Since it's a warm day and the snow is fresh, our skis won't slip that much."

Elliott was eager to impress his grandfather, and he felt confident he could make the run. His grandfather pushed off and began to make gentle turns. Elliott followed.

They arrived at the top of the Hundschopf, and Elliott peered down the steep, rocky incline. The racecourse had been prepared and groomed, and it was possible to ski down the area around the rocks. Several skiers had gone before them, some managing to make short careful turns and others sliding to the edges of the trail. Clive could see the apprehension in his grandson's face. "We'll ski down the left side of the trail, making short turns or snow plowing if you need to," he explained. "When we get to that area," he said, pointing to a spot with his ski pole, "we'll make a sharp right turn and then another left. From that point, it will be easy. Ready?"

Elliott nodded. His grandfather headed down the steep trail, making short, controlled turns. Elliott followed, maintaining good control. Clive reached the edge of the trail and made a sharp right turn and then a left. He skidded to a stop and watched Elliott, who followed. Elliott made the first turn admirably, but caught an edge making the left turn, and stumbled. He landed near Clive's feet and stopped.

"Well done," Clive said. "That's not an easy section. Look at the others," he added, noting several older skiers falling left and right.

Elliott brushed himself off, stood, and glanced up at what they had traversed. He wished he had made it without falling, but the fall was insignificant and only inspired him to try harder.

"Are you hungry? We can ski to town."

Elliott nodded, smiled, and pushed off behind his grandfather, who began following the trail into the village. At one point, Clive stopped and stood at the side of the trail. Elliott stopped nearby. Clive glanced up, letting the sun warm his face. He looked across the Lauterbrunnen valley. Elliott thought his grandfather looked sad, troubled, pensive.

"What's over there?" Elliott inquired, noticing a village perched on a bluff with massive peaks behind it.

"Mürren."

"Mürren?"

"Yes, it's another ski village. See that area over there?" he asked, pointing to a large area of snow fields.

"Hm hmm."

"That's the Schilthorn."

"Can you ski there?" Elliott inquired, squinting his eyes.

"Mürren has a lot of trails, and they are planning to open a cable car to the Schilthorn."

Elliott's eyes widened as he contemplated what would be quite a series of runs from such a lofty peak.

"How do you get to Mürren?"

"It's complicated."

"Can we go?" Elliott asked excitedly.

The question seemed to trouble Clive, who twitched. "No. There's enough for us here."

Elliott stared toward Mürren – another mountain waiting to be explored and conquered. He focused his eyes and identified trails cut in the forests, hugging the village. He wanted to go. He decided one day he would.

Elliott glanced over at his grandfather, who seemed captivated by the views of Mürren, almost frozen in place. He lingered a while, staring off into the distance. He was somber, not his usual jovial and gregarious self. Abruptly, Clive looked down at his hands, replaced his gloves, wrapped the pole straps around his wrists and said, "Shall we?"

They skied into Wengen along a trail that wove through houses, barns, and shops. Some villagers walked along the path on their way to work or to the market. Skiers navigated carefully through the narrow space. Once in the center of the village, Clive and Elliott removed their skis and walked on the pedestrian snow packed road. A few horse-drawn sleds passed. Some carried tourists, but others made deliveries of merchandise — food, wine, firewood, and building materials. The car-free village was enchanting.

Clive seemed to know his way, carrying skis on his shoulders, and walking deliberately through the village. On the other side of town, they approached a small inn, leaned their skis against a wooden fence, and walked inside the front door, making a turn to the left to enter the restaurant.

An elderly woman greeted them. "Mr. Williams, welcome back. And who is this handsome young man?"

"My grandson. Elliott."

"Nice to meet you. I'm Greta. Welcome."

She gestured for them to take a seat near one of the large windows overlooking the snow-covered road. She brought them menus. Soon, she returned with a beer for Clive and hot chocolate for Elliott. Clive ordered a schnitzel and Elliott a hamburger.

Elliott glanced around the room crowded with skiers taking a break and having lunch. He heard many languages and noticed all sorts of nationalities, although many of the patrons were English. Tables were separated by decorative woodwork, simple paintings of the Alps, and evergreens that had been put up at Christmas time. Outside the window, Elliott gazed up at the towering peaks and watched skiers slide to a stop at the edge of the restaurant. He thought it was so cool that there were no cars and that everything revolved around snow, skiing, and the breathtaking scenery.

"So, you made it down the Lauberhorn. That's quite an accomplishment," Clive said proudly, raising his stein of beer to Elliott's mug of hot chocolate.

Elliott blushed. He was proud of himself. "Can we do it again?"

"Hmm," Clive murmured. "Maybe tomorrow. Today, we should take the cable car up to Männlichen and ski down to Grindelwald."

Elliott grinned and let his feet rock under him with delight.

Their meals arrived. They were both hungry and ate with abandon. Elliott savored the burger, which was a rare treat. Clive squeezed some lemon juice on the schnitzel and cut into the tender veal. The smell of the dish brought back fond memories of earlier vacations in the Alps.

Greta walked past their table to check on them. She nodded and smiled. Clive took a deep breath, glanced at his grandson, and looked out of the window. Despite having grown up in England, he felt like this was home. He knew many of the locals who treated him like someone who belonged. He savored the local language, the food, the mannerisms and, of course, the astonishing scenery.

Once finished, they paid their tab and walked outside, grabbed their skis, and made the short walk to the cable car that would take them up the steep mountain to Männlichen. They lined up with other skiers and waited for the doors to open. Everyone rushed inside, eager to grab a place near the windows. Clive wedged his way to one side and let Elliott pass by so that he stood at the window's edge. Soon the tram began to glide along the cable heading up the mountain.

A few clouds drifted overhead, and it began to snow lightly. The scenery was breathtaking, with unobstructed views of the Lauterbrunnen Valley. At the top of the tram, they walked out onto a broad field of snow and secured their bindings.

"So, are you ready to ski back home? It's a long run."

Elliott smiled, nodding excitedly. "How long?"

"Oh, maybe five or six miles."

Elliott's eyes widened and his mouth opened in wonder. He had never skied that long of a run before. "Will we stop along the way?"

"Oh yes. I'm not a spring chicken, and I will need to rest a few times."

Elliott knew his grandfather was older, but he seemed invincible. He was energetic, affable, athletic, and in great health. Clive added, "Do you want to lead the way?"

Elliott hesitated. He didn't know the trails, and he was afraid they would get lost.

Clive noticed his apprehension and added, "In this area, we can take any number of trails, but they all end in the same area where we pick up the single trail to town. We can't get lost. You can choose whichever route suits your fancy. I'll follow you."

Elliott grinned, eager to take the lead. He pushed off quickly, glancing back to see if his grandfather had followed.

Elliott and Clive skied down the run, Clive watching his grandson carefully. The light had changed with the thickening clouds, and the snow began to fall more heavily. Clive knew it was easy for a storm to create whiteout conditions, and he hoped the heavy precipitation would hold off.

Elliott enjoyed the novelty of skiing while it snowed. Big flakes fell from the sky, dancing around them playfully. The groomed trail became softer, and turns were easier. Elliott felt more confident and skied more aggressively. Clive kept up but became nervous as he watched Elliott ski farther ahead.

Elliott stopped, waiting for his grandfather to catch up and take a break. They stood at the side of the trail near an old summer barn covered in snow. A thick forest of fir trees rocked back and forth in the wind. Elliott noticed Clive's concern and wondered if a storm was brewing. Elliott fantasized about getting caught in a blizzard - having to camp out in the barn, making a fire to stay warm, and returning to the village the next day, trekking through deep snow.

Clive said, "The weather is getting worse. We should continue down to the village. The sooner we get there, the better."

Elliott adjusted his gloves and poles and pushed off. They glided smoothly over gentle runs until the trail got closer to the village and steepened for the remaining section. Both maneuvered the complicated turns well and arrived at the terminus of the ski area and the little station of Grund. A train pulled up. They boarded and stood for the short five-minute ride to the center of Grindel-wald.

"Well, that was an adventure," Clive remarked as they walked toward the hotel.

"It was fantastic," Elliott replied, amazed at all they had skied and the varied conditions they endured.

They arrived at their hotel, stashed their skis in the ski room, and took the lift to their rooms. "I'll meet you later for dinner?" Clive asked. "Will you be okay on your own?"

Elliott was eager to assert his independence. "Of course, Grandpa. I'll take a bath."

"Good boy. If you need anything, I'm right here."

Elliott inserted the key into his room, sat on a wooden chair, and removed his ski boots. His feet were tired, but he was content with the day he had spent with his grandfather. He filled the tub with steaming hot water. He poured a little soapy liquid in and watched the bubbles foam on the surface. Soon he was reclining in the soft, warm water and felt his body relax.

After his soak, he dried himself, slipped on a robe, and laid on the bed, where he fell into a deep sleep. He woke to his grandfather's touch on his shoulder, announcing time for dinner.

Elliott quickly dressed, and the two of them went downstairs. The dining room was cozy with dozens of tables spaced carefully to create intimacy amongst guests. A maître d' winked at Clive and said something to him in German. Elliott thought he heard something like, "*Willkommen mein lieber Freund.*" The man rubbed his hand on Clive's shoulder and said in English, "And who is this handsome young man?"

"My grandson. Elliott. Elliott, this is Mauro, an old friend."

"It's a pleasure to meet you. I see you have inherited your grandfather's good looks!"

Elliott blushed. He thought his grandfather did, too.

Mauro sat them at the best table in the room and quickly filled their glasses with water. Then he asked, "*Das Übliche*, the usual?"

Clive nodded, glancing around the room. He noticed a few acquaintances and lifted his hand as if to say hello. It impressed Elliott that many knew his grandfather.

"So, young man, what would you like to eat?"

"Do they have schnitzel? With fries?"

"Of course, they do."

Mauro approached and paused at the table, placing a carafe of wine near Clive. Clive put his hand on Mauro's forearm affectionately and said, "Mauro, can we have two schnitzels with *frites*?"

"*Subito*, Mr. Williams," Mauro replied as he headed toward the kitchen.

"Isn't *subito* Italian?" Elliott inquired, curious as to the shift in language.

"Yes. You're very observant. It means right away. Mauro is from Italy."

"You speak Italian?"

"A little. Enough." Clive took an evasive sip of wine, not sure he wanted to get into a protracted conversation with his young grandson about why he spoke Italian.

"You speak German, too."

Clive nodded.

"How did you learn so many languages?" Elliott pressed.

Realizing he couldn't suppress his grandson's curiosity, Clive replied, "I've been around; crossed a few borders." He hoped the answer would satisfy a ten-year-old.

"I'd like to travel, too," Elliott remarked.

"Well, I think that can be arranged," Clive replied, scrutinizing his grandson carefully.

"Does grandma like to travel?"

"Yes. She does, but she's not crazy about skiing. Lucky for you. You get to be my ski companion."

"I miss her."

"Me, too."

"Can you teach me German?"

"Sure. Would you like to start now?"

Elliott nodded enthusiastically.

"When Mauro brings our food, you can say *Danke schön*. Or, if you want to use the local dialect, *Merci vilmal*."

"What's the local dialect mean?"

"It's a secret language that only people who live here speak."

Elliott's raised his brows and widened his eyes. "You mean, like spies?"

"Hmm," Clive murmured, feeling playful. "I guess so. It's like another world."

Elliott looked around the room, a room filled with people who didn't look like him or his grandfather. They spoke other languages and seemed to have a unique set of gestures and habits. He longed to join them; cross into another realm, one that seemed a lot more interesting than his own back home.

Their schnitzels arrived, and Elliott said, "*Danke schön*."

"*Bitte schön*," Mauro replied, winking at him. "*Guten Appetit*," he added.

Elliott beamed. He felt like an initiate, someone who had been welcomed into a clandestine world; one that was mysterious and full of allure. As he squeezed a little lemon juice on his schnitzel and grabbed a few fries, he realized his own world would never be the same.

After dinner, Clive and Elliott went into the hotel parlor to play cards by the fireplace. A handsome bartender brought Clive a glass of cognac and Elliott a Coca Cola. He was particularly attentive to them, stopping to ask if they were okay, and chatting with Clive in German.

At one point, Clive began to cough. Elliott looked up with alarm, and the waiter ran to get a glass of water, handing it to Clive. He sipped it carefully, and his cough subsided. In a raspy voice, he said, "I'm fine. Don't worry about me. *Mir geht es gut.*"

The bartender nodded and served some other guests.

"Are you okay, grandpa?"

"I'm fine. Nothing that a bit of mountain air can't cure!" he said, trying to conceal his concern as best he could.

They returned to their game and, suddenly, Elliott yelled, "Rummy," as Clive laid a card down on the table. They showed their cards, and Elliott raised his hands triumphantly.

"Well, well, well! If we don't have a card shark here," Clive said, winking at his grandson. He cleared his throat again. He was relieved that Elliott didn't seem alarmed by his coughing, and he hoped he wouldn't have another fit before they returned to their rooms.

"Another hand?" Elliott asked, taking a sip of his Coke.

"I'm afraid I have to go to bed soon. We have a big ski day ahead of us tomorrow, and I'm not as young and energetic as you."

"Oh, grandpa. You're the best. No one skis like you do."

"You're kind for saying so. I hope you had a good time."

"The best!"

"Shall we go upstairs?"

Elliott nodded reluctantly. Clive walked toward the bartender and shook his hand, placing his other hand on the man's arm. "*Merci vilmal,*" Clive said warmly, slipping him a few francs as a gratuity.

"*Bitte, gern geschehen!*"

Elliott walked up to the bartender, who seemed exceptionally handsome. He wore a white starched shirt, a vest, and dark pants. Elliott looked up at him – a tall and muscular man with blond hair and a friendly, playful face. He took a deep breath and said, "*Merci vilmal.*"

Clive and the bartender both chuckled and gave each other a quizzical look. Elliott was clearly a fast learner. Clive was both encouraged and a bit unnerved.

3

Chapter Three –
Allmendhubel

Mürren Winter 2007

On his way out of the Traumblick for his first day of skiing, Elliott slipped on some ice and stumbled off the front steps of the hotel, falling into a deep bank of snow. A family came out behind him, and he yelled, "Be careful!"

The man and woman took the hands of their two children and carefully navigated the slippery path.

"Are you okay?" the man inquired.

"Embarrassed, but that's all!"

The man reached down and helped Elliott stand. "Thanks," he said.

He brushed off his pants and jacket and tried to recompose himself.

Max appeared panting at the door, glancing down at Elliott. "Someone said there was an accident! Are you okay?"

Elliott blushed. "Yes. Just a little slip."

"Sorry. I should have put some salt on the steps." Max walked toward him. He brushed some remaining powder off the back of Elliott's shoulders and peered down at the back of his pants, still covered with snow. He was going to brush them, but he thought the gesture might be taken badly. "Here," Max said, handing Elliott his skis.

Elliott reached for them but then fell back, landing in the snow again. "Oh, my God. What a klutz," he exclaimed.

Max wanted to laugh, but he held back. He reached for Elliott and helped him up. The skis crossed and fell in opposite directions, with the poles bouncing farther away. Both tried to catch the falling skis but failed, each bracing themselves on one leg and holding each other with their free hands. Their eyes crossed. They laughed nervously.

Max remarked to himself that the obsessive-compulsive fussy businessman he had observed the evening before was capable of levity and mishap. He stared into Elliott's deep brown eyes and felt his legs grow weak. He tried to upright himself without jeopardizing Elliott's footing.

Elliott had already found Max handsome and charming and didn't mind that he was being held up by his muscular arms. Max took hold of Elliott's elbow and made sure he was standing securely. He then held his shoulders, patted them, and made sure he was firmly upright. "You stay here. I'll get the skis and poles."

Elliott blushed as he watched Max wade through the deep snow to retrieve his equipment. Max walked back with them and brushed the skis off. "Good as new," he remarked, holding them together as Elliott brushed snow off his jacket.

"Off for a day on the slopes?" Max inquired.

"It wouldn't seem like it, would it?" Elliott replied, chuckling.

"Need any suggestions?"

"You mean on how to walk?"

Max laughed and said, "No. Suggestions for ski terrain."

"Where is the beginner area?" Elliott asked, tongue-in-cheek.

"In all seriousness, if you want to warm up, you can take the Allmendhubel Funicular up the mountain. There are nice gentle runs from there to the village. Another nice area is Winteregg with longer runs. You can reach those from the top of Allmendhubel."

Elliott thought Max must not have had a lot of confidence in his skiing ability. He pressed him, "What about Birg or the Schilthorn?"

"Hmm," Max murmured, not sure how to respond. It was never a good idea to make guests feel inadequate. He glanced up at the sky. "It's a sunny day, but the temperatures are cold. It can get slick up there. But if you want to go, the Birg cable car is just down the road here."

"Maybe I'll take your advice and warm up first."

Max nodded, relieved.

Max handed him his skis, and Elliott took his time making sure he was on firm ground before he grasped hold of them. "Well, I guess I'm off."

"Have a good day!"

Elliott nodded and walked toward town.

Max brushed himself off, reached into a tin bucket at the side of the front entrance, and threw some salt onto the steps. He shook his head as Elliott walked up the hill. Inside the hotel, Sofia pretended to be busy. She looked too busy. As Max entered and noticed, he said, "You saw all of that, didn't you?"

"You guys were like Laurel and Hardy. I hope he's not going to the upper slopes!"

"I suggested he try Allmendhubel and Winteregg. You know, to warm up."

"Seems like a nice guy," Sofia said unconvincingly.

"He seems pretentious and uptight. Did you notice his table last night? Everything was perfectly organized, aligned, clean, neat. He seemed irritated at the noise," Max noted.

"Well, it was rather rowdy last night."

"We cater to families. I don't know how he ended up here."

"Well, he's here. Let's make him feel welcomed."

"What do you think I was doing out there helping him get up?"

Sofia didn't respond. She seemed troubled, preoccupied, perhaps even alarmed. She returned to her work, and Max went to the kitchen.

Elliott walked to town and found the entrance to the funicular. He read that it was a historic train, one built in 1912. Some of the earliest ski tourists in Europe came to Mürren, particularly the British. He entered the terminus, climbed a few steps, and took a place inside the car. Once the interior was full of skiers, a bell rang, the cable tightened, and the train began its ascent. As it reached a higher elevation, the funicular entered a tunnel before finally exiting at the top of the small mountain.

Elliott walked out onto a level area where people were putting on skis. He pivoted in place, taking in the magnificent scenery all around him. To Elliott's north and south, a variety of gentle trails led off through farmland and forests. Elliott leaned back and gazed at the towering peaks to his west. A cable car was approaching Birg, high above him. He felt vertigo just watching it slowly enter the station, perched precariously on a rocky ledge. From Birg, another cable car went even higher to the Schilthorn. Although a good skier, he was grateful for some gentle trails to get started. It had been a while since his last ski trip. He turned back toward the train station and noticed the village below. It looked like a postcard – a small hamlet filled with wooden chalets and historic hotels overlooking the Lauterbrunnen Valley. On the other side of the valley, Elliott noticed Wengen. He spotted the Lauberhorn Race trail, a ribbon of white that meandered down the slopes into the car free village. He had gone there countless times over the years with his grandfather, who always seemed unsettled as he gazed across the valley at Mürren, never wanting to visit. Elliott recalled vowing to ski there one day, and here he was! Feeling a knot in his stomach, he realized how long it had been since he last saw Clive.

Elliott stepped into his bindings, adjusted the straps of his poles, and made sure his helmet was secure and goggles in their right place. He pushed off and felt his skis glide on the soft snow. The runs from Allmendhubel were not challenging, nor were they long. He skied on a trail toward Winteregg to take advantage of a longer lift and lengthier trails.

The voice of his grandfather echoed in his head. "Lift as you transition from one turn to the next. As you begin to move into the turn, put your weight on the outer ski. Keep your shoulders and upper torso facing downhill. Point your poles where you want to make the next turn."

Elliott made graceful turns down the mountain. He took the Winteregg lift and skied down several trails. The slopes were full of children. He chuckled at their adroitness – at their seemingly effortless descents and turns. When he was growing up, skis were longer, harder, and the equipment more cumbersome. These kids didn't know how fortunate they were with comfortable boots and shorter curved skis that almost turned themselves.

At the bottom of the lift, Elliott held back and waited for older skiers to ride up with. He chatted on one ascent with a man from Bern, a retired politician. He reminded him of Clive — distinguished, in good shape, and a skilled athlete. The man spoke English and told stories of the good old days, before fancy lifts, modern equipment, and warm, dry clothing. He was curious to learn of Elliott's grandfather and wondered if he might have met him ages ago.

It didn't take long for Elliott to feel the effects of his hiatus from skiing. His legs began to ache, and he felt sweaty from the strain of so many turns. He found a quaint hut with unbelievable views of the surrounding mountains where a leathery man served beer, sausages, and melted cheese on pasta. He sat at a simple picnic table, removed his helmet, and let the warm sun caress his face. He breathed in the crisp, clean mountain air, and took in the views.

After lunch, he made a few more runs, glancing up at the higher slopes he hoped to tackle the next day. He eventually made his way to the village and walked back to the inn.

Sofia was standing at the reception area when Elliott pushed open the door. She looked up and raised her brows. "Mr. Williams. Welcome back. How was your day?"

"Magnificent. What a beautiful ski area."

"We're lucky."

"Did you grow up here?" Elliott inquired curiously.

"Yes. Max and I are both from here."

"Are most of the people who work here locals?"

"It's a mix. There are a lot of old families, like us, who have been here forever."

"It must be nice."

"We enjoy it."

"Well, I don't want to keep you. I'm heading upstairs."

"It's no bother. I'm not that busy. Where did you ski?" Sofia asked, eager to assess their single guest a little more.

"I went up to Allmendhubel, then to Winteregg, and finally to Schiltgrat."

"Wow! You covered a lot of territory!"

"I'm hoping to go up to Birg and the Schilthorn later in the week."

Sofia's eyes widened. After what she saw in the morning, she wasn't sure Elliott was up for the more challenging slopes. She nodded politely. "I'm sure you'll have fun."

"Well, excuse me," Elliott said, turning and taking the steps to the third floor.

That evening, at dinner, Max casually strolled by his table. Elliott had changed into his starched shirt, a ski sweater, slacks, and loafers. His book was, as usual, carefully aligned with the grain of the table. Nothing was out of line – the silverware, vase, candle, and placemat were all carefully spaced on the surface.

Max rolled his eyes. He swallowed hard, nodded to a few adjoining tables, then pivoted toward Elliott and asked, "Mr. Williams. How was your day on the slopes?"

"Call me Elliott, please."

Max looked at him impatiently, waiting for him to respond to his question.

"It was a great day. The conditions were splendid, and the variety of terrain is impressive."

Max wasn't sure that was the case. Mürren was not an extensive ski area, but he would humor his guest. "Yes, there's a lot to offer here."

Elliott glanced up at Max and nodded, snickering to himself about what would have been a great pickup line at a gay bar. "By the way," he asked. "Do you have any recommendations for après-ski?"

Max always considered the term après-ski a pretentious one. He cocked his head and glanced across the room, looking pensive, as if he was giving Elliott's question some consideration.

He turned toward Elliott and said, "Not really. This is a rather quiet town. Mostly families. A couple of the larger hotels have bars in their lobbies, but it's not like going out in Wengen or Grindelwald to a club."

"Hmm," Elliott murmured. "And if I wanted to go to Wengen, how might I do that?"

"It's complicated. There's the reverse route you took to get here – via Lauterbrunnen and Grütschalp, but the connection back to Mürren ends rather early. From Lauterbrunnen, you can take a bus to Stechelberg and then the cable car to Murren, but it's a roundabout way. It's really not practical to go to nearby towns at night from here."

"Hmm. So, what does one do here?"

Max wanted to say, sleep. Most parents were exhausted after a day on the slopes with their kids and couldn't wait to put them to bed and crash themselves. Elliott was an odd guest, and Max didn't know how to respond.

"Hmm, not sure."

Elliott squirmed in his chair, picking up on Max's frustration. "Well, thanks," Elliott said, a little perturbed.

Dinner was served, and Elliott was content to read, sip wine, and try to ignore the din of noise and activity in the room. The menu that evening included mushroom chicken scallopini, rice, and peas. Dessert was carrot cake.

Max observed Elliott from a slit in the kitchen door. He continued to worry about their new guest, concerned he would be unhappy, share critical reviews, or check out early, asking for a refund. He felt like he had to do something and finally walked out into the dining room as coffee was served.

"Mr. Williams," he began.

"Elliott."

"Elliott. I feel bad that there isn't much nightlife here in Mürren. Can I offer you some brandy in the parlor after dinner?"

Elliott looked around the room.

Max noticed his concern and said, "Don't worry. They will all be in bed and asleep in an hour."

"I don't want to bother you. I can take care of myself."

"It's no bother," Max said, unconvincingly. "It's the least I can do."

"Well. That would be nice," Elliott said, intrigued by the idea of spending some time with the handsome innkeeper.

"Will Sofia join us?" Elliott asked, in part as a courtesy and, in part, out of curiosity about whether he might have Max to himself.

"Oh, she's not a drinker, and she has lots to do at the end of the day. But thanks for considering her. *Bis später?*"

Elliott nodded and said, "Yes. Thanks. Until later."

He finished his coffee and dessert and casually made his way to the parlor. Someone had added logs to the fire as the flames were leaping up and the resin in the logs was crackling.

Max walked into the room from the kitchen and dining area. "Brandy?" he asked.

Elliott nodded, scrutinizing the handsome innkeeper who had changed into a sporty sweater and dark jeans.

Max reached under a credenza and pulled out two crystal snifers and a bottle of Remy Martin. He poured two generous glasses and handed one to Elliott. "*Salute!*"

"*Salute,*" Elliott replied. They both took long sips. Then Elliott added, "You have a nice place here."

"It's been in our family for several generations."

"I'm sure it must be a lot of work."

"It's manageable."

"You seem to do a nice business," Elliott noted.

"A lot of repeat families."

"I must be an odd guest," Elliott suggested.

Max raised his brows. He hadn't expected Elliott would be even remotely self-aware. Maybe he wasn't as pretentious and demanding as he appeared. "I have to admit I was stumped when you arrived alone, particularly given the room you booked."

"I've been wanting to come here for many years. The Traumblick was on a postcard I discovered in my grandfather's belongings."

"Ah. That's how you found us. I was wondering."

Elliott nodded. He observed that Max suddenly relaxed his shoulders. He had been sitting on the edge of his chair, and he now slid back, crossed his legs, and stared into the fire.

Elliott seized the opportunity to take a more protracted look, hoping Max wouldn't sense he was scrutinizing him. Max looked like he might be roughly fifty. He was fit for his age – a lean body, probably because of a lot of work and exercise in the mountains. His salt and pepper hair glistened in the orange light, and his face was luminous. As he leaned toward the fire, his muscular back pressed against the fabric of his shirt.

Max turned toward Elliott. Max's hazel eyes sparkled. "So, what do you do in England?" he asked.

Elliott hoped Max didn't detect the craving in his eyes. All his life, he took notice of men - of their physiques, their gestures, and clothing. He always feared they would notice him undressing them with his eyes and become angry or hostile. More importantly, he feared if they noticed, he would have to admit that he desired them, wanted them, preferred them. Even after coming out, the same recording played over and over in his head.

Elliott looked away as if in thought. While staring at the fire, he casually replied, "I'm an architect."

"What's your specialty?"

"Homes."

"We'll have to get you to do some work for us here?" Max said, not really serious about the offer. Furtively, he glanced at Elliott's hands and noticed there were no rings.

"I'm not sure Alpine structures are my forte," Elliott replied, glancing around at the room and its décor.

"We can coach you."

"Hmm," Elliott murmured, unnerved by Max's sudden warmth and friendliness. He continued, "And you? Did you ever consider another profession?"

"The inn has always been in our family. I entertained the idea of studying medicine, but the practicalities of life caught up with me, and I remained here."

"Any regrets?" Elliott asked. He realized the question was probably too personal and checked himself, adding, "Sorry. Perhaps that's too personal of a question."

Max nodded no. He glanced back toward the fire. Almost imperceptibly, he murmured, "No. Not really. I enjoy my life here."

"It's a magnificent place." But Elliott couldn't imagine living in such a small, isolated village. He'd go stark raving mad. He loved to ski, but there would have to be more.

Elliott noticed a painting on one of the walls. He stood and walked toward it. It was a beautiful rendition of a winter scene – a ski trail passing a wooden barn covered in snow with blue-gray snow-covered peaks in the background. It reminded him of a day on the slopes with his grandfather. As he stood admiring the painting, Max took the occasion to take an inventory of Elliott's assets. He was tall and broad shouldered. Although he dressed more formally than most at the inn, there was a playfulness about him – the free flow of his hair and the errant tail of his shirt lying on the curve of his buttocks. Max took a long sip of his brandy, hoping to dampen the unruly thoughts coursing through his mind. Elliott frightened him, annoyed him, appealed to him.

Although he knew the answer already, Max asked, "Any children?"

Elliott nodded no and continued to examine the painting. Then he said, as if to throw Max off-course, "At least not yet."

Max thought to himself, "He'd better hurry." But he imagined Elliott was not in a hurry; perhaps he never wanted kids.

Elliott wanted to ask the same question, but presumed it was a sore subject. He was certain Sofia and Max had to have tried. The idea of passing the inn to the next generation must have been an expectation. He pivoted and walked toward the sofa facing the fireplace. Max sat on the large chaise to the right. Elliott took a seat and stared into the burning embers. "This is nice," he said pensively with a warm smile.

Max twitched nervously and took another long sip of the brandy. He thought it was nice, too. He craved male companionship, and Elliott was more pleasant than he had anticipated. But what did Elliott mean by his statement? Did he like the ambience – the fire, the inn, the brandy – or did he enjoy having a warm conversation with him, with Max? Max felt blood rush to his face, and he perspired nervously. He gulped down the rest of his brandy and stood abruptly. "Well, I hope you will stay and enjoy your drink and the fire. I have some chores to finish before bed."

"Oh, I'm sorry. I didn't mean to keep you," Elliott interjected, unnerved at Max's abrupt decision to leave.

"It's not a problem. I'm sorry there aren't more social opportunities here."

Elliott felt his stomach tighten. Had Max seen through him and felt the need to dissuade him with a not-so-concealed statement about the lack of opportunities? How horrible, he thought to himself. Had he become the creepy guest owners have to set boundaries for? He hoped he hadn't annoyed or alarmed Max.

He tried to disarm any potential tension. "Don't worry. Maybe this is what I needed."

Max looked nervous and raised his brows.

Elliott clarified, "You know. A quiet respite. A time to read and ski."

Max sighed. To Elliott, it looked like a sigh of relief. Max then said, "Well. Stay here as long as you like."

"*Vielen Dank,*" Elliott replied, unnerved at the quick ending of their post-prandial.

"*Gute Nacht.*" Max said as he nervously made his exit to the kitchen.

4

Chapter Four – Margrit's Note

Grindelwald Winter 1970

Elliott slipped on his long underwear and stepped into his ski pants. They were a new model – slim and form fitting. He had a new blue jacket with black sleeves that made it look as if he were wearing a vest – a very cool look; he had to admit. Elliott gazed at himself in the mirror. He had grown another two inches in the last year. His chest had filled out, and he had let his wavy dark hair grow longer. He tilted his head and gazed into the mirror at the emerging dark beard that had formed on his face, lining his jaw and circling his mouth. At eighteen, he had lost his adolescent awkward look and had become a handsome young man.

He went downstairs to retrieve his and Clive's skis. Clive was still skiing, but he was slower in the mornings, and it helped if Elliott carried things for him. Clive appeared as the elevator door opened and smiled at his grandson.

"Ready?" Clive asked Elliott.

Elliott nodded. "I've got our skis. Do you have your gloves and goggles?"

Clive checked his equipment and nodded. They walked the short distance to the station and caught the first train to Kleine Scheidegg, joining hordes of skiers who pushed their way into the train cars.

Since he was ten, Elliott had been coming with his grandfather every couple of years to Grindelwald to ski. He had grown familiar with the resort - with its trains, lifts, and trails. It had been two years since his last trip, and he was eager to conquer the mountain.

People were talking excitedly about the day. The sun was shining, and fresh snow had fallen. It was a holiday in Switzerland, so the train was filled with young local people. Elliott had taken German lessons and was eager to listen in - to make sense of the surrounding conversations. He glanced over at Clive, who had on a dark pair of sunglasses, and gazed out of the window at the passing scenery. He seemed lost in thought.

Even at 75, Clive was in great shape. He exercised regularly, took care of himself, and always had the newest ski fashion and equipment. Elliott caught an older woman sitting near them observe Clive. Clive turned toward the center of the train and noticed. He smiled warmly at her, but then glanced away, gazing, instead, at the tall, athletic men standing in the aisle.

Elliott had become more sexually curious over the past couple of years. Just the year before, the Stonewall riot in New York had set off a wave of curiosity about homosexuals. A few of his classmates came out, causing a great raucous at the school. Elliott hadn't really given much thought to sexual orientation before, but now he found himself second guessing his assumptions as he observed people, including his grandfather.

Elliott's grandmother had passed just three years earlier. Marie and Clive seemed to have had a warm and happy marriage. There was nothing that suggested to Elliott that his grandfather was anything other than a happy and healthy heterosexual.

But now that Clive was single, Elliott had questions. Did a 75-year-old experience sexual attraction? Might his grandfather fall in love again? If so, with whom? Who did his grandfather find attractive? Elliott began to observe Clive more carefully, wondering if he had missed something before.

Clive was friendly and warm to everyone – men and women. But he had a certain reserve around women. When he was younger, Elliott assumed Clive's reserve was a way of remaining faithful to his marriage. Now that he was a widower, Elliott wondered if he continued to treat women with a certain distance out of habit or out of a sense of guilt for having survived his wife and not wanting to substitute her with someone else. Or was there something more to Clive's reserve, another narrative he had overlooked?

Elliott watched him gaze at the handsome men in the train aisle, scanning their clothing and equipment. His gaze lingered, uncomfortably so. Most would nod at him out of respect, an older skier they undoubtedly admired for his stamina and endurance. Clive was an inspiration and had a way of conveying encouragement to those around him with a warm smile, a nod of the head, or a compliment about ski equipment.

Elliott found himself gazing at the same men. He studied their outfits – the beautiful sweaters with alpine designs woven into the fabric. Several glanced his way. They were handsome, with broad chests, powerful legs, and alluring eyes. He found their gaze unnerving, as if they saw something in him, something he hadn't recognized himself; a craving that simmered below the surface. He wondered if his curiosity was simply that or if there was more to it?

The thought of it being more terrified him, and he glanced down evasively at his boots, fussing nervously with one of the buckles.

They arrived at Kleine Scheidegg after a forty-minute ascent through forests and snow fields. The north face of the Eiger Mountain towered over them. At the station, everyone disembarked and headed briskly to a flat area where they fastened skis. Some headed toward the Lauberhorn lift and others skied down to Arvengarten.

"Shall we go over to Männlichen today?" Clive asked.

"That sounds like a great idea," Elliott said enthusiastically.

Clive led as they skied down a gentle trail toward Tschuggen, a lift that would take them up toward the edge of Männlichen. They took the T-bar up, where a magnificent vista of mountains and slopes spread out below them. There had been talk of adding a gondola from town to Männlichen, but nothing had been built yet.

"Shall we do some fresh powder?" Clive asked of his grandson.

Elliott looked down the slope. The snow was deep and powdery, but he didn't have much experience skiing off the groomed runs. He hesitated. He gazed over at his grandfather, eager to tackle the pristine terrain.

"I'll follow you," Elliott said, hoping he might get into a good rhythm by watching his grandfather ski ahead of him.

Clive pushed off and seemed to float in the powder. Elliott wondered how his grandfather had perfected skills for skiing off-piste. Elliott did well at first, managing to make relatively smooth turns left and right. But, at some point, he let his skis go too deep, and he flipped, falling face forward in the deep snow.

Clive continued down to the groomed trail and waited for Elliott to brush himself off and catch up.

"Maybe we should stay on the designated trails," Clive suggested.

"How do you do it?" Elliott asked, admiring his grandfather's skills.

"I let gravity do the work," he said with a twinkle in his eye.

"It doesn't seem to work for me the same way," Elliott replied.

"You've got to keep your chest facing forward, downhill. Keep your knees bent and let the skis float on the top of the snow."

"I tried that."

"The secret is keeping your torso facing downhill. It's counter-intuitive when you begin to gain speed. But it's the only way to stay in control – face the steepness, face your fear."

"Hmm," Elliott murmured as they pushed off onto the groomed trail and made their way down to the next lift.

On the way up the lift, Elliott remarked to his grandfather, "I can't believe we are here again. Thanks for inviting me."

"My pleasure. But it's part selfish. Your father won't let me go alone anymore. I need a chaperone."

"I think it's the other way around," Elliott remarked, certain his father would never let him travel to a ski resort without Grandpa Clive.

"Well, then. We are two chaperones in search of trouble!"

They both chuckled.

"You're so inspiring," Elliott said to his grandfather. "I want to be skiing when I'm your age."

"If you don't use it, you will lose it. I try to keep active."

"Well, you're amazing."

Clive blushed. He glanced up the hill in front of them and became pensive. What really inspired him was the fear of losing his vitality; the fear of losing the appeal that had been the force behind his one true love, the one that had gotten away. He clung tenaciously to the idea that if he kept himself in good shape, there was always hope, always the possibility of a reunion, of a reconciliation even if the other had already passed. He realized it was irrational, but at least it worked. At 75, he was still skiing with his teenage grandson.

After a few runs, they skied down to the village and caught the train that would take them back to Kleine Scheidegg. Once there, to Elliott's surprise, Clive wanted to take the taxing Lauberhorn T-bar to the top. But, at the top, he said, "I think I need to take a break. Shall we ski toward Wengen? There's a pleasant restaurant on the trail."

Elliott didn't want to waste a minute eating. He was eager to ski all day long, but he knew at 75, Clive had reached his limit. "Certainly, Grandpa. I'm hungry, too."

They skied on the first part of the Lauberhorn race run and then took an easier trail through a beautiful forest. The filtered sunshine created a dappled effect on the surface of the soft snow. They came to a clearing and a restaurant with a nice terrace overlooking the Lauterbrunnen Valley. They skied up to the building, took off their skis, and approached the hostess, who found them a nice table on the terrace in the sun. A server came, took their orders, and retreated to the kitchen.

"This is amazing," Elliott said, glancing over the valley. "I never tire of the views. Isn't that Mürren on the other side?"

Clive twitched nervously. He stared across the expanse, his eyes sullen. He nodded, but without enthusiasm.

"In all the years we've been coming here, we've never gone over there. Why not?" Elliott asked as the server returned with their drinks.

Clive took a long sip of his beer. He didn't look up.

"What's wrong Grandpa?"

"Oh, nothing," Clive replied, faking a smile, and nodding at other patrons around the deck.

"I know when something's troubling you. What's wrong?"

"It's a long story. I'm not sure I'm up to it."

"It's our first day of skiing, and we should take it easy. We have plenty of time."

Clive took a long sip of his beer. His head hung low. He seemed deep in thought.

"So, grandpa, why don't you want to go to Mürren?" Elliott asked thoughtfully.

Clive cleared his throat, paused, and then said with a raspy voice, "I've been there before - a long time ago."

Elliott's eyes widened, and he raised his brows in anticipation of what promised to be an intriguing tale.

"When?"

"During the First World War."

"What?" Elliott exclaimed, wondering how his grandfather had ended up in the Alps during the war. Stories about the war were always shrouded in a cloud of mystery. Clive rarely talked about those years. He wondered if his grandfather had been a spy or something.

"Yes. During the war, the Swiss took in prisoners and housed them in resort hotels."

Elliott glanced over at Mürren and then back at his grandfather. He found it hard to believe that the beautiful Alpine village in front of him had been an internment camp for prisoners.

Clive continued, "It was a way for the Swiss to keep their tourist industry alive and make sure prisoners had humane care. They took in French, Belgian, British, and German prisoners."

"And you were a prisoner?" Elliott asked, now certifiably intrigued.

Clive nodded.

"You never talk about it."

"It was a sad time."

"How were you captured and how did you end up there?"

Clive paused. He wasn't sure how to answer or what to recount. He felt his chest tighten. "Well, they captured my battalion in France."

Elliott could only imagine the terror of being in the trenches and seeing the Germans come for you. "Were you injured?"

"Minor. I and a few of my unit were the lucky ones. They killed most of the others."

"It must have been horrible," Elliott said.

"It was. You can't imagine." Clive rarely thought back to his time on the battlefield. He had been an idealistic twenty-one-year-old, ready to defend England and the rest of Europe from the German aggressors. But what he found in France was beyond belief – a chaotic sea of trenches, mud, barbwire, and carnage – bodies lying everywhere. At night, light breezes blew smoke and the stench of rotting bodies across the field into their camp. Even now, from time to time, Clive thought he smelled the troubling odors in his nostrils and on his clothing. It was a haunting memory.

"So, how did you end up here?"

Clive paused, troubled by the images that had formed in his mind. Then he began slowly, pensively. "First, they sent us to a camp in Germany. We were crowded onto trains and taken deep into German territory. During the journey, we thought at any moment they would take us out of the carriages and shoot us. We weren't convinced we would end up as prisoners."

Elliott's eyes widened. "What happened next?"

"The conditions in the camps were horrible. We were cold and wet. I developed trouble breathing and had a persistent cough. Influenza and TB were rampant."

Elliott recalled that his grandfather periodically suffered from respiratory stress.

Clive continued pensively, "The camps became full, and the Germans began looking for ways to ease themselves of the burden of caring for us. We learned that they negotiated a deal with the Swiss government to take some of us in. I was one of those chosen and was soon on a train to Mürren. On arrival, the medical team confirmed that I had tuberculosis as well as unhealed wounds from shrapnel. There was a group of us assigned to a hotel specializing in heliotherapy."

"What's that?"

"They believed that the crisp mountain air and intense sunshine would help clear tuberculosis. We laid in the sun on a protected terrace for days on end."

"Did it work?"

"Yes. I got much better."

"What was it like in Mürren?"

"Compared to the camps in Germany, it was paradise. We had nice accommodations, good food, and opportunities for exercise. We weren't locked up so we could study, work, and socialize. But it wasn't all pleasant."

"How so?" Elliott inquired.

"Well," Clive began, rubbing his chin. "It seemed unending. We were there for several years, not knowing how the war would end and what would eventually unfold. A lot of my comrades grew weary and suffered breakdowns."

"Did they torture you?"

"Heavens no," Clive replied excitedly. "The Swiss were very caring. But toward the end of the war, heating and food supplies grew limited. People were worried. Some of my comrades succumbed to their wounds or underlying maladies. It was stressful since no one knew how things would end."

The server came with their meals. Elliott was starving and eagerly consumed his hamburger. Clive seemed lost in thought. He pushed the fries and veal stew around on his plate and took a few small bites of the food.

Between bites of his burger, Elliott glanced over at Mürren, trying to imagine the early part of the 20th century. It had to have been more primitive and remote. And he couldn't imagine what it was like to live during a time of so much carnage. "You said you had injuries. What were they?"

"Some shrapnel in one of my legs."

"Which one?" Elliott asked, looking under the table at his grandfather's legs.

"This one," Clive said, extending his left leg out from under the table. He pointed to several places up and down his shin. "If it had hit me higher, I might have died or had more disabilities."

"Does it hurt?"

"Only when I overdo it," he said, grinning, holding his hand up to his mouth as if caught red-handed.

"Does it hurt to ski?"

Clive looked off into the distance. He nodded yes and murmured, "A little."

"Oh, Grandpa. We don't have to do this."

"Of course we do. It is what inspires me. There was a group of us during the war who hiked and skied all over this region. Some had lost legs or had injuries far worse than mine. Watching them overcome their disabilities motivated me. In their honor, I vowed I would ski until I died."

"So, you skied there, in Mürren?"

"Yes. That's where I learned. There was a British man who had been exempt from military service – an Arnold Lunn. He ran several hotels in Switzerland. He taught us and organized excursions and races. Lunn is often considered the father of British skiing."

"And you knew him?"

"We were friends."

"Is he still alive?"

"Yes, but we've lost touch."

Clive took a bite of his lunch and Elliott wiped his mouth clean after finishing his burger. He took a sip of beer and glanced back across the valley.

"So, why don't we go to Mürren? You could show me where you learned to ski and where you stayed."

"It's too painful. I couldn't bear it," Clive admitted.

"I'm sorry," Elliott said, not sure what burdens his grandfather carried from the time he spent there. Then he asked, "So, when the war was over, you came home?"

Clive's face twitched, and his eyes watered. He just nodded.

"And you married grandma, right?"

"Yes, a couple of years later. She was so beautiful and smart and thoughtful."

"Where did you meet?"

"At a dance. The church sponsored socials and dances for young people to meet."

"And you met her there?"

"Yes," Clive said, drifting off in thought. He didn't say anything for a while. He turned back to Elliott and said, "She was incredibly understanding."

Elliott gave his grandpa a quizzical look. He wasn't sure what she had been understanding of, and he was convinced Clive didn't want him to ask or probe.

Suddenly, Clive said excitedly, "Let's change the subject! How are you doing? How's school? Any romantic interests yet?"

Elliott blushed. He didn't have any romantic interests. He was shy and lacked confidence. "No one in particular. I'm still young."

"I know, but you have eyes. You must have noticed people. And I'm sure they've noticed you!" he said, winking at Elliott. His grandson was handsome, athletic, and smart. It wouldn't be long before he was snatched up!

"How old were you when you and grandma married?"

"Well, let me think," Clive began. "When we married in 1920, I would have been twenty-five."

"Anyone before grandma?"

"Oh, so we're back on me again?"

Elliott nodded and chuckled. His chin was resting on the back of his hand, and he stared at his grandfather, who seemed restless, unable to focus on eating or on the train of conversation. "Anyone before grandma?" he repeated the question.

Clive squirmed in his chair and looked down at his beer. Elliott thought he saw a tear forming in his grandfather's eye. There was a long, quiet pause. Finally, Clive said, "No. No one."

Elliott wasn't convinced.

"And how old were you when you went to war?"

"Twenty-one."

"So, no one before that?" Elliott was convinced there must have been a girl before his grandmother, someone who had made the moves on his handsome grandfather.

Clive was more emphatic. "No. Certainly not."

"It must have been incredible when the war ended and people returned home."

Clive looked lost in thought. Suddenly he turned toward Elliott and asked, "What did you say?"

"It must have been a relief to head home."

Clive nodded pensively.

"Did you go back to school?"

"I wanted to study law, but I was too old to start that. I ended up getting a position as a manager for a company and worked my way up."

"Business management, right?"

Clive nodded.

"You've done well."

"Yes, I guess you could say that. I can afford nice vacations to Switzerland, can't I?"

Elliott and Clive chuckled. Elliott was Clive's only grandson, and he had benefitted from Clive's generosity and affection over the years.

They finished their meals. "Shall we head to Wengen and take the cable car to Männlichen? We can ski home from there."

"Are you up for it?"

Clive nodded.

They stepped off the terrace and walked to the fence where they had left their skis. They tossed them on the snow, stepped into the bindings, and took their time skiing into the center of Wengen. At the terminus for the tram, they unbuckled their skis and took their places in the cable car. Soon they were floating in mid-air, rising to the peak above. They had places by the back window, and Elliott observed his grandfather. His face was pressed against the window, gazing out at Mürren in the distance. A couple of tears formed in his eyes and ran down his cheeks.

As they continued their ascent, the town receded from view. Clive wondered how many more times he would visit the area and if this might be his last view of Mürren.

Back in Grindelwald, Elliott helped his grandfather get settled in his room. He had stowed their skis in the ski room and helped Clive get out of his boots. "Can I get you something to eat or drink before we go to dinner later?"

"No. I'm good. I'm going to take a bath and then do some reading. Why don't you take a walk into town? Maybe you will meet people your own age. I hear there are a couple of après-ski bars that are quite active," he said, winking.

"Grandpa!" Elliott exclaimed in protest.

"It will do you some good," Clive asserted. He retreated to the bathroom and ran some hot water in the tub.

Elliott looked around the room. There were socks and shorts lying about, so Elliott began to tidy things up. He threw out some chocolate wrappers and washed some dirty glasses. As he dried them and placed them on the dresser, he noticed a few books and some letters. He wondered what his grandfather was reading. He was always up to date on political affairs and social issues. A couple of postcards caught his attention. They looked like alpine scenes. While his grandfather was getting ready in the bathroom, he picked one up. On one side, there was a beautiful photograph of Mürren - one of the town center - with facades and eaves of wooden hotels overhanging a snow-covered pedestrian road. Skiers were gliding along between buildings, and a few kids were dragging sleighs.

Elliott turned the postcard over. The return address was the Gasthof Traumblick and dated December 1965. The note was in an old form of German script. Elliott couldn't read it, but the end of the note was signed "Love Margrit." He held the postcard in his hand, rubbed his fingers over the script, and wondered what it meant. Given the sadness his grandfather seemed to have for Mürren, he wondered if he hadn't left broken-hearted, if he hadn't indeed had a girlfriend before his grandmother.

Chapter Five – Teenage Affections

Grindelwald Winter 1970

Max had turned sixteen earlier in the month and was eager to go out to bars. His great uncle, Niklaus, lived in Grindelwald and invited him for a long weekend to celebrate his birthday and give him a chance to take advantage of what Grindelwald had to offer in contrast to the quiet town of Mūrren.

Max slipped on a new ski sweater, dark slacks, and leather boots. He slicked back his dark hair, spritzed a little cologne on his collar, and headed eagerly out of the door of his great uncle's chalet, at the edge of the village. It was snowing lightly, and Max's boots made a crunchy sound as he walked on the snow-covered path into the business center.

His uncle recommended several bars, but his friends at school tipped him off to a less-known establishment that catered to young foreigners. He had been studying English, and he wanted to meet tourists from abroad.

As he walked down the main street, he noticed lights from the club casting a yellow glow on the snowy pavement, promising a warm welcome. He approached the front door and could hear loud music. His heart raced with excitement.

He walked in and glanced around the crowded space, an antique wooden structure decorated with ski posters and antlers from mountain goats. A large U-shaped counter surrounded by bar stools dominated the center of the room. Along the outer walls, there was a narrow wooden shelf where people placed steins of beer as they visited.

During the last couple of years, he had accompanied his great uncle to clubs and had learned the routine. He made a broad circle of the room, giving the appearance of looking for someone in particular. His uncle said it was a good way to survey the crowd and identify opportunities.

A well-dressed international clientele enjoyed après-ski drinks before dinner. Max found a strategic seat at the corner of the bar and ordered a beer. He was nervous and wished he had come with friends or even his great uncle, but he was determined to make the most of his first evening on his own at a bar.

As his classmates promised, the room was full of foreigners – mostly English, but there were also Dutch and Germans. The cacophony of languages and variety of nationalities created a cosmopolitan vibe – an intoxicating sense of being part of something greater than oneself, a youthful camaraderie that transcended borders, politics, and historical antipathies.

A tall, dark-haired English guy wedged his way past Max toward the counter to order a drink. The guy smiled apologetically to Max. Max couldn't help noticing his dark brown eyes and the confident way he leaned against the counter. He wanted to try out his

English but froze. He just nodded to him, feeling an intense heat emanating from the guy's body.

As the man waited for his beer, he pivoted toward Max. Max felt his legs grow weak and wondered what that meant. The guy seemed interested in starting a conversation and said, "*Hallo. Ich heisse Elliott.*"

Max extended his hand and quickly replied, "*Max. Möchtest du hier setzen?*" He gestured for Elliott to take his seat as he slid over to the adjacent bar stool.

Elliott nodded and took a seat next to Max and said, "*Merci vilmal.*"

"*Bist du Engländer?*" Max asked as Elliott grabbed his beer, toasted Max, and took a sip.

"Is my accent that bad?" Elliott asked in English, chuckling nervously.

"No, your German is good. I was just curious. I'm trying to practice."

"What are you practicing?" Elliott asked, smiling playfully at Max.

"English," Max said as he felt blood rush to his face. While he wanted to improve linguistic skills, he realized this was his first time in a bar alone, and he needed to practice the art of meeting people and engaging in clever conversation. His classmates bragged about meeting girls, flirting with them, and getting a kiss before heading home. A few noted that if one were lucky, one might get close enough to graze a girl's tits or place hands on her bottom.

He and Elliott sat close to each other and glanced evasively at the crowd, neither knowing what to say next. They both began at the same time, "Are you here skiing?"

They chuckled. Elliott gestured for Max to continue. "I live in a nearby village. I ski all the time," he said.

"That must be amazing. I only come here from time to time with my grandfather."

Max looked around, as if expecting an older man to appear. "And where are you from in England?"

"Yorkshire, north of London."

Max nodded, as if familiar with the area.

"You know it?" Elliott asked.

"I know of it. I've never been," Max replied, not sharing the fact that he had not traveled much. But since he worked in the family inn, he was familiar with British towns associated with their guests.

Elliott peered into Max's hazel eyes. They sparkled in the ambient lighting. He felt something stir in his chest.

Suddenly, a couple of women walked past them, giggling as they sipped their straws. Elliott glanced in their direction and followed them with his eyes. When he turned back toward Max, Max was staring at him, not at the girls.

Elliott realized Max was handsome. He had a robust frame, playful hair, and a charming smile. He assumed the women had spotted Max. They were making a second pass already. They slowed as they approached. One looked over at Elliott and winked as she took an evasive sip of her cocktail.

Elliott felt self-conscious. Even though everyone told him he was handsome, he couldn't imagine that two attractive international women – seemingly from Holland or Denmark – might pick him out of the crowd. Elliott followed the other woman's eyes toward Max and noticed he seemed even more uncomfortable than Elliott felt himself. Elliott decided to take the initiative. "*Hallo.* Do you want to join us? There's room here." Elliott said, gesturing that they could make space near the bar for the four of them.

The two women glanced at each other, nodded, and pivoted toward Max and Elliott, edging their way toward them and the bar. "Can I offer you another drink?" Elliott asked them.

"Yes. Very *gentil*," one of them said in broken English and French.

Max detected their Dutch accent and asked them in Dutch, "Are you from Holland?"

They both smiled excitedly and sighed in relief. One of them replied, "*Sprichst du Deutsch?*"

Max glanced at Elliott, who nodded affirmatively to Max, who then said, "*Natürlich.*"

The two women, Ida and Anna, introduced themselves, everyone shifting to German. Elliott was the least fluent but held his own. They were on a ski holiday with their respective families. Ida was more talkative and Anna more flirtatious. She was stunning - with a slim but shapely body, shiny blond hair, and dreamy blue eyes. Ida was not as beautiful, but she had expressive eyes, dark brows, and a luscious mouth.

The four of them chatted about Grindelwald, skiing, school, and their favorite musicians. Elliott took care of one round, and Max another. Ida and Anna eventually excused themselves to meet their families for dinner. Max and Elliott remained longer, eager to process the fortuitous evening.

"Wow," Elliott began as Ida and Anna walked out of the door. "They were fantastic."

Max nodded, but not enthusiastically. He glanced around the room nervously, as if looking for an exit strategy. In fact, he had been obsessing over Elliott during the evening, watching how his mouth pursed with various words, the casual gestures he used in response to Ida's and Anna's flirts, and the way he spoke with his expressive eyes. He felt his reserve was melting, and he feared what he might do if Elliott gazed into his eyes.

Elliott was awkward around women, and he felt triumphant that Ida and Anna had spent considerable time with Max and him. He wondered if their brief encounter had been an anomaly or something he could repeat. Glancing around the room, he searched for more social opportunities, but didn't notice any other unattached young ladies.

After scanning the room, he turned toward Max and noticed him nervously looking around. Able to peer at him undetected, Elliott was struck by Max's intensity, as if thoughts and emotions were swirling heatedly under the surface. He had a raw masculine aura that Elliott found exciting, even a bit intoxicating.

Max pivoted toward Elliott, catching his eyes. Elliott was tall, handsome, and seemingly self-assured. For a Brit, he spoke German well and had an enchanting ease to him. While Elliott's allure frightened him, Max didn't want the evening to end and feared Elliott would soon excuse himself for dinner. "Another?" Max offered Elliott.

"Thanks. Sure," Elliott said, glad Max didn't want the evening to end prematurely, either. Max ordered two more beers. Both had quite a buzz, and they were riding the euphoria of the night.

Elliott gave a more protracted look at Max. Earlier, he seemed inscrutable and shy. He had become more gregarious and relaxed with the beers they had consumed. He could imagine them being chums, skiing together, going out to clubs, and traveling around Europe. Max was handsome and cute, playful and pensive. The idea of having a chum from a foreign country who spoke another language was appealing, even a bit exotic. How many of his friends back in Yorkshire could boast about that?

As they drank their beers and swayed to the top hits blasting from the jukebox, Elliott found himself scrutinizing Max's body - his hips and buttocks swiveled independently from his formidable torso, and he had cocked his head back, apparently savoring the liquor, the music, the crowd. Max seemed oblivious to his allure, to his charm, and Elliott found Max's innocence mesmerizing.

Elliott leaned against the bar facing the large room. He set his beer down on the counter and placed his hand casually on Max's shoulder. It was an unusual gesture for someone from England — a country used to formalities and reserve. But Elliott felt he was part of a modern generation, one where affection could be shared across genders, and he felt at ease and comfortable with Max, his new Swiss buddy.

Max melted at Elliott's touch, at the warmth emanating from his hands and filling his chest. He felt himself stir, and he trembled. He wondered if Elliott had penetrated his thoughts or had seen the craving written all over his face. The intensity of Elliott's hand on his shoulder frightened him, and he casually slid away from Elliott, pivoting away from the room and toward the bar to take a long evasive sip of beer.

Elliott followed Max's lead, turning toward the bar, too. He leaned his elbows on the counter and pressed his left arm against Max's right arm and leaned his shoulder into Max's shoulder. Elliott took a sip of his beer and set it back down on the counter. "This was a fun evening. I'm glad we met."

"Yes. It was fun. *Es hat grossen Spass gemacht,*" Max said with minimal emotion. He began trembling as Elliott pressed up against his shoulder. He tried to control his body, but it betrayed him, a spontaneous and visceral reaction to Elliott's touch and proximity.

Elliott could feel Max's shaking and gazed toward him. Max's eyes were filled with terror, turning red and watery. Not sure what was happening, Elliott leaned away from him and said, "*Entschuldigung.*"

Max shook his head, as if there was nothing to apologize for. He lifted his beer to his mouth, hoping the alcohol would calm him, but now his hands were unsteady as well. Embarrassed, he feared Elliott could see the desire in his eyes, and now, with his body shaking, it would be impossible to conceal.

Elliott detected Max's discomfort and felt terrible that he had done something that offended him. He wondered if his affectionate gesture had frightened him or made Max think that he was gay and making a pass. He had enjoyed their bantering and the camaraderie they had shared, but now he wondered if Max had interpreted it differently and was about to hit him out of anger. Elliott glanced down at Max's fists; they were closed tightly.

"*Wollen wir gehen?* I have to get back to my grandfather," Elliott interjected quickly.

Max nodded, relieved. He sighed and handed the bartender several francs.

Both grabbed their coats from the hooks by the door and walked outside into the crisp, cold air. There were a few flurries dancing in the light cast by the streetlamp. Max shuffled restlessly in place as Elliott looked up and down the main street to orient himself. Both were tense.

"I'm going this way," Max said, pointing away from the center of town toward his great uncle's home.

"And I'm going the other direction," Elliot added, nodding toward the train station and his hotel. "It was nice to meet you."

Max smiled timidly. He realized he had lost control, had let frightening and painful emotions overwhelm him. He both hoped and feared that Elliott might share contact information with him. Elliott had picked up on Max's ambivalence and decided not to make Max any more uncomfortable. "*Alles Gute*," he said, wishing Max the best.

Max said, "Have a good ski vacation. Maybe we will run into each other sometime."

Elliott nodded but said nothing more, realizing it was unlikely they would run into each other. He walked toward the hotel to meet Clive for dinner, his head lowered as he carefully navigated snow and ice on the slippery sidewalk. He had hoped his evening would have been a triumph, connecting with other young people from around Europe and testing romantic waters. Ida and Anna had been a pleasant surprise, but he couldn't shake the haunting feeling he had for Max and the unsettled emotions in his stomach over their abrupt and untidy farewell.

Elliott was well-liked, and he never had a friend tell him off or walk away from him. He was in new territory, and it unnerved him that he had failed miserably with Max. He feared Max thought he was gay. Surely his generation could be freer expressing affection and fondness without it having to be interpreted as anything more. His father was reserved and cold, much like his peers. He wanted to be more like his grandfather, someone comfortable expressing fondness and warmth to a variety of people and genders. That didn't mean he was gay, he reassured himself. But Max's reaction alarmed him, and he vowed never to make that mistake again.

6

Chapter Six – The Archives

Mürren Winter 2007

It was snowing heavily. Elliott had returned to his room after breakfast. He checked the webcams, and even at higher elevations, visibility was zero. On his way back from the dining room, he noticed the parlor was filled with kids playing cards, board games, and running in and out of the front door, covered in snow. He decided a quiet day in his room on the top floor might be a good idea.

He pulled a comfortable stuffed chair toward the window, wrapped himself in the quilt that covered the bed, and reached for a couple of books he had brought to read during his vacation. One was about European banking, but that didn't seem like a good option for a snowy day. He had another book, a romance novel. It sounded perfect. He opened it and settled in for a relaxing read.

Around 10, Sofia knocked on the door, piercing the soft quiet that had descended everywhere as heavy snow piled on the roof and the landscape outside. "Come in," Elliott said.

"Sorry to disturb you. Here are some towels, and I can straighten things up for you."

"No need," he replied.

She glanced around the room. Everything was in its place, just as she expected. No guest had ever been so fastidious. She walked toward the bathroom and replaced the towels. She pulled a bar of chocolate out of her apron and set it on the dresser. "In case you get hungry later."

"I'll probably take a walk into town if the snow lets up."

Sofia looked out of the window. The snow was blowing horizontally in a stiff wind. The trees at the edge of the property were hardly visible. "Hmm, probably not," she noted.

"Well, thank you for the towels."

Sofia cleared her throat and stood in the doorway. She clearly had something on her mind, something she wanted to say or ask. Elliott looked over at her and asked, "Is there something the matter?"

She nervously nodded her head no. Then she slowly began to voice a few words. "It's just, I hope you aren't disappointed in our inn."

"Why would I be?" Elliott asked, although he realized that having chosen the Traumblick was probably a mistake. There wasn't enough to do at the inn or in town.

"It's just, you know, we tend to have mostly families with kids as guests. I can't remember the last time we had a person like you, someone who was single."

Elliott stared at her curiously. In reaction, she held her hand up to her mouth and said, "Oh, I'm sorry. I didn't mean it that way."

"What did you mean?"

"I'm sorry. Perhaps you aren't single. I just meant someone unaccompanied."

"Don't worry about it," Elliott said, glancing down at his book. He was increasingly irritated at Sofia's awkward statements. He hoped his focus on the book would be a hint that she should leave. She remained. She took a deep breath and asked, "Do you have kids?"

Elliott nodded no. Sofia was quiet and sullen. He wondered if the question came from her own sadness at not having kids. He felt a sudden sense of compassion for her and said, "I'm not married either."

"I'm sorry."

"Don't be. I was married but now divorced. It's for the best."

"Hmm," she murmured, even more curious. "So, what brings you to Mürren?"

"Skiing."

"But why a quiet town like this?"

"I've always heard it was a nice place."

"Have you skied other resorts in Switzerland?"

"Wengen, Grindelwald, Verbier, Zermatt."

"Wow! I didn't realize."

"You must have seen my clumsiness yesterday," he said, sensing she couldn't imagine him skiing other major resorts.

Blushing, Sofia chuckled and nodded.

Elliott felt his body become warm. Blood rushed to the surface of his skin. He realized that perhaps she had seen him scrutinizing Max. He thought her questions might be territorial. With all the guests coming and going, she and Max both must have seen a lot, witnessed a lot, and been objects of suggestive invitations and innuendos.

"What do you do back home?"

"I'm an architect."

"Ah," she said. "And where did you learn to ski?"

"Mostly from my grandfather. He loved this area."

"And why the Traumblick?"

"My grandfather had some postcards from here. I wanted to come, and I recognized the name of the hotel."

"Your surname is common. What was your grandfather's first name?"

"Clive. But I don't think he ever came here to ski."

Sofia gave him a curious look. Elliott didn't elaborate.

"Well, I hope you have a pleasant stay."

"Thank you. You and Max have been very accommodating and warm."

Sofia's face flinched. Elliott noticed. She cleared her throat again. "By any chance, do you have the postcards that mentioned our hotel? I'm always curious to see what's out there, what kind of images are in circulation."

Elliott sighed, annoyed that Sofia was taking up precious reading time. He wanted to get rid of her, so he rose, walked toward his suitcase, and pulled out an envelope. "Here. This is one of the postcards that mentions the Traumblick."

Sofia took the card and glanced at the photo of the town. She turned it over and saw the note in German. Sofia scanned it quickly and held her hands up to her mouth, saying, "Oh my God, this is a note from Margrit. She's my great grandmother."

Elliott furrowed his brow. He knew it was signed, "Love Margrit." He thought Margrit must have been a woman Clive came to know during his internment, most likely someone he had become fond of, perhaps even loved. He didn't realize there was any connection between the hotel and its owners.

"I never had the note translated. It's in an old cursive script. Even with my basic German, I can't make out much. Do you know what it says?"

Sofia cleared her throat and said thoughtfully, "It's a note to your grandfather about my great grandfather's death in 1965. Hans."

Dismissively, Elliott said, "There must have been a lot of people who knew each other from that time. My grandfather was a prisoner here during the First World War."

"Ah. That would explain it. Hans was a doctor who cared for the soldiers."

Elliott was now intrigued. He raised his brows and looked off into the distance, formulating some questions in his mind. He turned to Sofia and asked, "Do you know much about that time? Was your great grandfather alive when you were younger? Did he tell you stories? I'd love to know more."

"I was young when he died. I don't remember him talking about it. But my grandfather, who was born at the beginning of the war, would sit around the fireplace, look at old photographs, and share stories that Hans had told him."

Elliott gestured for Sofia to have a seat. "Tell me more."

"I don't know where to start. Did your grandfather talk about his time here?"

"Only once, and not in any detail. He didn't like to talk about the war, and he seemed particularly reticent to talk about Mürren."

"Hmm," Sofia murmured. She glanced out of the window and felt a chill pass through her. She continued, "I would have thought his time here was good. From everything I read and heard, the prisoners were given good care. Was he sick?"

"He had some minor wounds, but from what he told me, nothing serious."

"And he never came back?"

"Not that I'm aware of. He took me to Grindelwald and Wengen to ski, but he adamantly refused to come to Mürren."

"That's very strange. I wonder what happened?" Sofia asked.

"I have no idea. I just know that whenever he glanced toward Mürren or made a comment about it, there was sadness."

"I'm sorry to hear that. What is your grandfather's name again?"

"Clive. Clive Williams. Why do you ask?"

"Just curious."

But it was more than curiosity. Sofia fidgeted in her chair. "I'm sorry to have disturbed you," she stated. "I need to get back to my chores."

"Not a problem," Elliott said, glancing back down at the book he was eager to take up once she left.

Sofia stood, tucked some linens under her arms, and left the room. She ran quickly to the attic. While most of the reports of prisoner care in Switzerland were positive, from time to time, an archive or old story would appear that raised some doubts. Some believed unauthorized experiments took place. Others alleged that some injured soldiers were forced to work for more food or were exploited for other purposes. She worried that her great grandfather had done something nefarious, perhaps to Clive. She hoped that wasn't true.

The Traumblick had a large attic filled with boxes of memorabilia from four generations. She pushed newer boxes to the side and found several rusty iron cabinets against a dusty back wall. Someone had put a small piece of masking tape on the front drawers with the notation: Hans Weber. Medical Files. World War 1.

She pulled on the top drawer, and it was stuck. She shook it forcefully several times, and it sprung open. Inside, she found countless files dated 1916-1918 with names of British soldiers. Alphabetized, she realized Elliott's grandfather would be one of the last files. She tugged open the lower drawers and finally found a file marked, Williams, Clive.

She opened it and scanned the notations that had been made over the course of nearly two years. She ran her fingers over the old script, closing her eyes and imagining her great grandfather holding the very same documents in his hands. Much of the information was coded in medical jargon. Between the old script and the specialized vocabulary, Sofia strained to make sense of the notes.

At the end of the first year, she observed that the notations were mostly positive. She made out phrases such as "no more symptoms," "has gained weight," "skis with colleagues," and "requires no more therapy." It appeared that Clive came for checkups on a regular basis.

She thumbed through the remaining pages and then gasped for air at what she read. Toward the end of the file, just as the war had ended, the notations changed. She held her hand up to her mouth and whispered, "Oh my God." She quickly replaced the file, closed the cabinet, and left the attic, securing the lock on the door. If what she suspected was true, it was no accident that Elliott was a guest at the Traumblick.

7

Chapter Seven – The Arven
Hotel

Mürren November 1918

Hans made the short walk from the center of town to the Arven, a charming hotel at the edge of the village with enviable views of the Jungfrau. It was snowing heavily, the start of winter. He had invited Clive to meet him there.

Fresh tracks in the snow suggested Clive had preceded him, had perhaps already let himself in. Hans approached the front porch, pushed open the door, and glanced inside. "Anyone here?"

There wasn't an answer, but he sensed someone was inside. He walked into the parlor. There were no lamps on, but bright gray light poured in from a large window. "Doctor Weber," Clive said with a velvety voice, moving toward the center of the room from a side wall where he had been glancing at some art.

Hans didn't respond. He walked up to Clive and stared longingly into his eyes. Clive wanted to give Hans a kiss, but he had learned that Hans didn't respond well to direct and open affection.

It took time, clever conversation, and an accidental touch to melt his reserve.

Clive felt himself stir. He always did. Hans was an unfathomable and mysterious man. While not tall, he had a robust frame with a large head, playful dark hair, and a sexy mustache. His eyes were deep and intense. His forehead was broad, and he had a thick nose with a luscious curvature.

In clinical settings, Hans was talkative and inquisitive. In Clive's presence, he was oddly at a loss for words. Emotions swirled just below the surface - feelings he feared expressing.

In a deep voice, Hans uttered, "Clive."

Hans' voice was tender and warm, and when he pronounced Clive's name, Clive felt himself melt. He nodded, almost imperceptibly, and said in reply, "Doc. It's good to see you. It's been a while."

At first, Hans didn't respond. He was gripped by Clive's allure, by the distinctive coloration of Clive's face – a blend of darker olive tones with shades of rouge and crimson on his cheeks. Clive always appeared flush, aflame – a furnace of thoughts and desires fighting for release.

Hans raised his hand as if about to caress Clive's temple. He checked himself and said simply, "It's good to see you, too. *Ich habe dich vermisst.*" He missed seeing Clive since the war had ended and routines had changed.

"You said you wanted to show me something?" Clive asked, staring into Hans' eyes.

Hans nodded and walked toward a side table, where he struck a match and lit a small oil lamp. An orange glow filled the wood paneled room. He beamed as he looked around the space.

"My new acquisition," Hans replied with a smile. His eyes were still fixed on Clive, whose face was luminescent in the orange light.

Clive returned a quizzical look. "Are you buying the inn?"

Hans nodded, glancing around the room.

"Really?" Clive asked, raising his brows.

"Yes. I've grown fond of Mürren and always admired this place on my walks. The owners needed to sell. I got it for a good price. What do you think?"

"Well," Clive began hesitatingly, "it's nice. Rather charming and cozy." He pivoted in place and began to take note of the decorative walls, the stone fireplace, the fine carpets, and the crystal lamps. "But what do you know about inn keeping?"

"Nothing. That's why I want to show you the place."

Clive grew alarmed.

"Let's take a look."

Clive didn't respond.

They walked into an adjoining room, and Hans lit another lamp. "This is the dining area."

"It's large. Spacious." Clive pivoted in place. The room had a large window that opened toward the mountains across the valley. It was snowing, and the ethereal view of the mountains was enchanting. Clive added, "It's beautiful."

"I'm going to give the inn a new name – the Gasthof Traumblick – for the views!"

"Hmm," Clive said as he walked through a maze of tables toward the window to take in the dramatic landscape. He turned back toward Hans, who was fussing with a loose piece of molding along one of the dining booths.

"And the kitchen?" Clive inquired.

"Follow me," Hans said, walking into an adjoining white tiled room. He lit another lamp. Copper kettles and pots hanging from the ceiling began to glow in the light. Hans ran his hand over several large ovens next to which were stacked freshly cut logs for fuel.

"Impressive," Clive said.

Hans smiled contently. He walked up behind Clive and observed his dark wavy hair glistening in the flickering light of the wall lamp. He wanted to touch him and share his excitement. The voice inside his head began to remonstrate himself for troubling, wayward desires. Hans reached around Clive to rearrange some large spoons in a canister, one of countless pretexts Hans had become a pro at inventing in order to graze Clive's arm or accidentally press against his solid body.

Clive turned and felt Hans' hand slide past his waist. Their eyes met in the dim light.

"It seems well-equipped," Hans said, raising his brow. Clive wanted to chuckle at Hans' double entendre, but he had grown annoyed by the games Hans played, had been playing for the last year.

"And this is the best part," Hans began excitedly, leading Clive down a dark hallway. They turned a corner and entered a sizable room. Hans lit a lamp and light filled the space. There was a sofa, some comfortable stuffed chairs, and a fireplace over which hung a beautiful painting of the mountains in the summer. "This is the owners' suite. There's a nice family room, a private bath, a large bedroom, and two smaller rooms for children."

"Ah," Clive said, nodding as he walked through the apartment. "It seems perfect for you," he said with an edge of resentment.

Hans picked up on Clive's prickliness. "Do you want to see some of the guest rooms?"

"I think I've seen enough," Clive replied, eager to learn more of Hans' plans.

"Oh, come on. They are nicely decorated and have splendid views."

Clive sighed, realizing it would be difficult to dissuade him.

Hans walked briskly out of the suite into the front reception area and then up the wooden stairs to the third floor. He pushed open a door and walked into the bright room. "This is one of the biggest guest rooms. It is a mini suite with a sitting area, private bath, large bed, and enviable views of the Jungfrau. See?"

Clive walked toward the large window. The snow continued to fall heavily, covering the nearby peaks with a frosty white coating. He had to admit that the views were breathtaking. Another winter season was descending upon the region. He had grown to love winter. He had learned to ski with several buddies, and there was something about the coziness of fireplaces and warm companionship that he cherished during the cold weather. But the war had just ended, and life was now an open canvas. As he gazed into the swirling snow, he wondered where life would lead him.

"Come feel the mattress," Hans said, having already sat on the bed.

Clive turned around. He nodded no. He already knew what was to follow.

Hans patted the space next to him. "Come on."

Clive sat reluctantly.

Hans reclined. "Ahh," he said as he fell back onto the soft mattress.

"Feel it," Hans continued, reaching for Clive's arm and pulling him back.

Clive collapsed next to Hans. The mattress was billowy, and the white and red quilt covering the bed felt soft. He turned toward Hans, who faced him with playful and ravenous eyes. He glanced down at Hans' crotch and noticed he was hard. Clive imagined Hans' firm sex in his hand and felt himself stir.

Hans was, as usual, quiet. He peered into Clive's eyes. He reached over and unbuttoned Clive's trousers, an action that he performed robotically since his eyes, his mind, his thoughts were focused on Clive's alluring brown orbs. Hans played tricks in his mind. He couldn't think about what he was doing. He pretended to be seized by an overwhelming force, something that snuck up on him, something he hadn't intended but which he allowed to unfold, nevertheless.

Hans played with the fly of Clive's trousers, as if they were two school-age chums casually toying with each other. Clive became aroused, and Hans let the back of his hand slide over the hardness underneath the fabric. Soon, Hans reached inside Clive's undershorts and took hold of him, and Clive began to moan. He had learned not to say anything or express his affections. Hans needed to follow the spontaneity of his body, a force that was out of his control, one with its own mind and intentionality, not his. He couldn't be held accountable for what he was about to do.

Clive felt Hans' hand fumble with several buttons on his shirt as he opened the fabric and slid his hands inside. Hans' hands were always warm and soft. Clive felt them glide across his pecs, as they had done during numerous examinations before. Hans adroitly ran his hands back down to Clive's erection and rubbed the soft moist end, throbbing with excitement.

Hans was sufficiently aroused that Clive could now take hold of him without any protest. There would be remorse later but, at the moment, Hans was aflame and couldn't turn back. Clive leaned toward Hans and gave him a long, warm, moist kiss. He felt Hans' heart pound next to his own and reached around Hans' back and took hold of his round, firm buttocks. He slid his hands inside Hans' trousers and felt the soft skin. Hans moaned.

Hans turned onto his back. Clive knew this was an invitation for him to slide his hands inside Hans' trousers and take hold of him. He did. He felt the hot skin in his hand and stroked it. Hans writhed in pleasure. Clive rubbed the end of Hans' sex and then ran his fingers along its side, pressing down around his scrotum and between his legs. Hans screamed, "*Oh, mein Gott.*"

Clive slowed his hands, carefully timing things. If Hans came first, he would collapse into a sea of regret and let go of Clive. Clive knew he either had to come first, or they would come together. As he slowed his movement, Hans increased his, taking firm hold of Clive and squeezing him. Clive felt his skin become moist, his muscles contract, and his buttocks clinch.

Clive peered down at their bodies, pressed close against one another. Hans was lighter and smoother; Clive was darker and had a thin coat of hair covering his muscular chest. Hans had strong legs that Clive loved to massage with one hand as he worked Hans with the other.

Clive felt the supple glide of Hans' hands move up and down him. Despite Hans' reserve around sex, Clive had grown fond of him. He was intelligent, insightful, caring, and full of wonder. Hans inspired Clive to dream big and to embrace the world.

He loved the way Hans transported him to another place, one of mystery and intrigue. As Hans moaned, Clive listened attentively to the strange words Hans uttered as he gazed at him – *gutaussehend, deine dunklen Augen, gross und hart.* He knew what they meant, even though his German was rudimentary. Only one glance into Hans' eyes, and Clive could feel his heart expand. He felt handsome and powerful in Hans' hands. Soon, he felt the customary waves of pleasure course through him and explode in a powerful climax.

He glanced over and noticed Hans close his eyes. He had traveled to another world - aroused and excited. Clive wondered where he was and who he fantasized about. Hans held himself with one hand and, with the other, ran his warm fingers along the inside of Clive's legs. They pressed into Clive's muscles. He hoped it was him; that Hans wanted him, that Hans loved him. He watched Hans begin to writhe as swells of pleasure gripped his body and he climaxed. As he did, Hans gave Clive one last squeeze of his leg. Clive sighed, content that Hans wanted him.

For a few quiet moments, they remained on the bed, bathed in the soft gray light of the winter outside. Hans stirred first, buttoned up his trousers and adjusted his shirt. He sat on the edge of the mattress. Clive pulled himself off the bed and dressed. He wanted a cigarette or a glass of brandy.

Hans looked at Clive with his customary compunction and shame - his head held low, his eyes sullen, and his shoulders rounded forward, burdened by the guilt he carried. Clive shook his head and rolled his eyes. Soon, Hans cleared his throat and said, "Well, shall we continue?"

Clive nodded incredulously. There were never words of thanks or affection after their exchanges. It was an emotional letdown, and he continued to tell himself that he should give Hans up. But during the heat of passion, as they enjoyed each other's bodies, Clive knew he was desired, and that he was handsome and irresistible. For the time being, that was good enough.

They continued touring the inn and finally returned to the parlor. It was cold.

"Shall I make a fire?" Clive asked, glancing at a stack of wood.

Hans nodded.

Clive took some kindling and carefully placed it on the andiron. He positioned some small logs on top and struck a match, holding it up under the twigs. Soon orange flames leaped from the smaller pieces of wood and began to singe the larger logs as resin crackled in the heat.

Hans searched through several cabinets and found an old bottle of whiskey. Hans poured them both a glass and they sat in comfortable chairs near the fire.

"So, what do you think?" Hans asked.

Clive was still thinking of the sex they had had. He savored the smooth taste of the whisky trickling down his throat. It was rare that they took a moment to savor their time together.

"Of the inn?" Hans pressed him impatiently.

"Well, it's beautiful, but are you sure you want to become an innkeeper? It's a special art."

"I'm going to continue my medical practice, but I'd like you to help — you know, manage the inn."

"I'm returning home."

"You don't have to. I can process papers for you to stay, work papers, since you would be essential to the local economy."

"And what about Margrit and Conrad?"

"What about them?"

"Well, wouldn't it be a bit odd for me to be hanging around here with them here, too?"

"You'll have your own place. I'm sure you will find a wife and start a family, too."

Clive felt a sharp pain fill his heart, as if a lance or sword had been pressed into his chest. He loved Hans, and he couldn't imagine marrying someone and pretending to be something he wasn't. Against all reason, he had hoped that perhaps Hans would come up with some kind of arrangement, a kind of understanding, where he and Hans could share a life. He didn't want to be the chum down the street or the manager at the inn.

Hans continued, "Soon there will be little Clives to play with Conrad and his brother."

Clive rolled his eyes, not really interested in fathering children. He gave Hans a curious look and asked, "Conrad has a brother?"

"Soon. Margrit's pregnant."

Clive felt his chest tighten. He stood. His face was red, and he felt anger building inside. He blurted out, "I can't do this?"

"What?"

"Be the housemaid who skulks about and waits for the innkeeper to push me into an empty room and have his way with me."

Hans looked evasively toward the fire and grunted. "That's disgusting."

"Of course it is. The war is over. It is a new age. I want to love you honestly and openly."

Terror raced across Hans' face.

Clive continued, "I love you. We are both young. We have a whole life in front of us."

"That's why this is perfect. You can stay here."

"No. You want me to get married, have a family, and work with you. It's all very convenient."

"It seems perfect."

"It's not. After we pleasure each other, you can't even look me in the eye. You can't tell me you love me. Do you know how that makes me feel?"

"You know I have deep admiration for you and treasure our time together."

"Can you say it? Can you say I love you?"

Hans squirmed in his chair and peered into the dancing flames in the fireplace.

"Can you?" Clive reiterated his question emphatically.

Hans didn't respond.

"I didn't think so. I've been wasting my time." Clive stood up.

"How can you say that?" Hans said, now turning toward Clive. "You mean the world to me. That's why I'm buying the inn. I want you to stay. I want us to be partners."

"What kind of partners? Business partners?"

"That and more."

"You have that with Margrit, with Conrad, and the rest of the children to follow."

"You'll have that, too."

"I don't want that. I want you," Clive said imploringly.

Hans turned toward the other side of the room, away from Clive, and murmured something to himself.

"Say it. Tell me you love me, and I will consider it," Clive said.

Hans stared into the fire, wringing his hands. He wanted to blurt out the words. He wanted to tell Clive he loved him, but it felt like a deep crevasse he couldn't traverse. Hans feared it would alter everything - things he couldn't face, things he didn't have the courage to change.

A door closed behind him. He looked out of the window and saw Clive walking briskly away.

Hans collapsed onto the floor and began to sob. He craved Clive. It was impossible to resist Clive's eyes, his firm, solid body, his playful personality, and the feel of him in his hands. He felt shame. As much as he tried to avoid temptation, he needed Clive. Clive made him feel alive, made him feel sexual, made him feel young and handsome.

The war seemed interminable, and it was only in recent months that the prospect that Clive would return to England hit him. He couldn't imagine his future without him. He thought his idea of buying an inn and having Clive work with him was perfect, but Clive's demand for a declaration of love was too much.

He realized he needed more time to convince Clive of his plan. He stood, extinguished the lamps, and spread the logs in the fireplace so they would soon quit burning. He closed the inn and walked outside.

He climbed the hill, following Clive's tracks in the snow. He walked into the center of town and entered the hotel where he had cared for British prisoners. Hans opened the door to his office. It was cold and dark. He lit a lamp, turned on a small gas heater, and removed his coat.

He walked to his desk and glanced down at the three stacks of files. One stack represented the most seriously wounded who had been returned to England months ago, before the war ended. German authorities knew they were incapable of returning to battle. It was cheaper to send them home early than to continue to provide care for them in Germany or Switzerland.

Another group included those who had fully recovered. Now that the war had ended, they could return home. Hans thumbed through the files, recognizing their names and medical histories - men he had cared for and nursed back to health. At the bottom of the stack, he took hold of the last file - Williams, Clive.

There was a third group of patients whose TB or wounds were persistent. Many had made progress, but there was concern if they returned to England, particularly with its cold damp climate, they would grow worse. British authorities were not eager to add to the public health burden at home and forced those men to remain in Switzerland for longer.

Hans opened Clive's file. He glanced through the notations going back two years. He recalled the first days he had examined him and smiled. Clive's humor, warmth, and good looks had been contagious, and it wasn't long before they became special friends. Hans ran his finger over the notes and remarked how quickly Clive had recovered from his leg injuries and how responsive he had been to the mountain air and sunshine. His TB was no longer detectable.

Hans sat down and took out a pen. He knew what he was about to do was unethical and dishonest, but he rationalized that TB rarely disappeared entirely from a patient. Although Clive was healthy, in all likelihood, the disease persisted or was dormant, even if undetectable.

Hans paused and looked off pensively into the distance. He felt adrenaline race through his body as he contemplated what to write on Clive's file, something he knew would change their lives forever. Dipping a pen in the ink well, his hands trembling, he noted, *Clive Williams has made remarkable progress over the last two years, but in recent months, there has been a return of symptoms in his chest. I was incredulous at first, but now I am certain that his TB has returned. Since he has responded so well to treatment here, it is my recommendation that he delay his return to England and remain during winter for more care.*

He let the ink dry, closed the file, and added it to the short stack of those who were to remain in Mürren.

He extinguished the lamp and heater, put on his coat, and walked outside into the swirling snow. Margrit was expecting him for lunch.

8

Chapter Eight – Grandfatherly Advice

Grindelwald Winter 1970

Mauro sat Clive and Elliott at a nice table by the window, where snowflakes danced in the outdoor lights of the hotel restaurant. Clive ordered some wine, and Elliott decided to take a break after having had several beers earlier in town.

"So, how was your evening out?" Clive began, eager to hear of his grandson's adventures.

"Nice," Elliott murmured, glancing at the menu. He wasn't sure how much he wanted to share with Clive and needed some time to process what had transpired.

Clive opened his menu and glanced at the specials for the day, pondering whether to go for a veal stew or perhaps an entrecôte done in green peppercorn sauce, one of his favorites. He noticed Elliott was quiet and prodded him more. "Did you meet anyone when you were out?"

The question startled Elliott, wondering if his grandfather was psychic or something. He continued to avoid Clive's glance, staring at the meal options before him.

Conveniently, Mauro appeared, placing his hand on Clive's shoulder. "Have you decided on what you want to eat yet?" he asked.

Clive looked over at Elliott, who nodded that he hadn't.

"Give us a few more minutes," Clive suggested.

"*Torno subito*," Mauro said tenderly to Clive, winking at him.

Elliott observed the casual affection between Mauro and Clive and remarked to himself how unremarkable and harmless it seemed. Mauro's and Clive's interaction seemed so easy and unassuming, in contrast to Max's alarm at Elliott's innocent touch earlier in the evening. Elliott remained unsettled at Max's apparent antipathy and wondered how his grandfather managed to express affection without eliciting similar hostility. Surely Elliott's generation was more enlightened.

"Do you know what you want?" Clive asked.

Elliott twitched in his seat, an unconscious and spontaneous reaction to Clive's question. He hoped Clive didn't notice, but he had. "I'm going to have the schnitzel. As usual," he said.

"Try something different," Clive prodded him.

"I like the schnitzel. You can't go wrong."

Clive creased his forehead and scrutinized his grandson. He asked, "So, did you go to the usual place for drinks? What's it called, the Ibex?"

Elliott nodded.

"Any interesting people?"

Elliott nodded.

"A man of many words tonight."

Elliott paused. "We met some nice girls from Holland."

Clive noticed Elliott had referred to a 'we,' but it was clear he wanted Clive to focus on the girls. So, he played along. "Were they cute? Friendly?"

Elliott nodded enthusiastically. "They were here on ski holiday with their families. Seemed like nice women. They are at the university."

"What are they studying?"

"Education or something like that."

"Ahh," Clive murmured. "Are you going to meet up with them later tonight or in the week?"

"We didn't make any plans."

"Too bad. You should seize opportunities when they present themselves. Life will pass you by very quickly."

Mauro came and took their orders.

Sebastian, the bartender for the hotel parlor, passed through the dining room and stopped at their table. "Mr. Williams and Elliott. Nice to see you. Will you be coming by later?"

Clive glanced inquisitively at Elliott. Elliott nodded. Quiet time with his grandpa was more appealing than a complicated evening on the town.

"See you later," Sebastian said, placing his hand casually on Elliott's shoulder.

Elliott felt the warmth in Sebastian's hand. It felt comforting. Sebastian disappeared into the restaurant kitchen and then reappeared, carrying a tray of glasses and plates to the parlor bar. He was a young man, perhaps in his twenties. Tall and of slim build, he walked with a certain elegance. He had playful dark hair and a sexy mustache that just covered the upper part of his round, boyish mouth. Elliott followed him with his eyes as he retreated to the main part of the hotel. When Elliott looked up, Clive was staring at him, having watched his grandson observe the young bartender.

Clive realized his grandson probably shared his proclivities, but he hadn't come to terms with them yet. His grandson was about the same age he was when he first realized he was different, and only a little younger than he was when he fell in love with Hans. He sighed and took a long sip of wine, fighting a war of jealousy and paternalism within himself.

"Sebastian seems like a nice guy," Clive remarked.

Elliott blushed, realizing his grandfather must have noticed his eyes. "Hmm," he murmured. "Yes. He seems nice. Everyone seems to like you."

"I've been coming here for a long time."

"You must know everyone well."

"Not everyone. But yes, I have gotten to know a few people over the years."

Later, Mauro approached, bringing their entrees. He placed Elliott's plate of schnitzel and fries in front of him, and then he placed the entrecôte with peppercorn sauce in front of Clive. "*Guten Appetit*," he said. "Is there anything else you need?"

"*Danke schön*," Clive replied, nodding his head no. Mauro retreated to the kitchen.

"So, Mauro. Is he married? Does he have a family?" Elliott inquired, curious to make sense of his grandfather's friends and their relationships.

"No. I don't think so," Clive replied, looking down at his plate and slicing into the tender steak.

"And Sebastian?"

"He's still young. Why do you ask?" Clive knew why he was asking.

"Oh. Nothing. Just curious."

"How's the schnitzel?" Clive asked, giving his grandson some mental space.

"Delicious!"

"These girls you met. Did you speak English or German?"

"German. Although Max and I spoke in English."

"Max?"

Elliott realized he had slipped and reached for a couple of fries to avoid Clive's inquisitive look.

"A guy I met at the bar."

"Where is he from?"

"Here."

"Nice guy?"

"Seemingly," Elliott said without elaboration. He reached over to the carafe of wine on the table and poured himself a glass, taking a long sip.

Clive noticed Elliott's nervousness. He yearned to come out to his grandson, to offer him advice, to help him avoid the mistakes he had made, but it would involve disclosing facts he had spent most of his life carefully concealing. Grindelwald was his happy place, a community of like-minded men who shared an affinity for each other but who, for professional and personal reasons, remained discreet. He owed it to Marie; he owed it to his friends.

Clive savored the camaraderie of the handsome men who served him, of the skiers he met at the après-ski bar, and the warmth and affection they shared with one another over a pint of beer, a brandy, or a cup of espresso. He wanted more, but the price of transgression was too high.

"So why hasn't Mauro married?" Elliott prodded his grandfather.

"I don't know," Clive replied without looking at Elliott.

Elliott found it hard to believe his grandfather didn't know more about Mauro. They were quite friendly and seemed to know each other well. It seemed odd – a single man of Mauro's age, unmarried. Elliott wasn't aware of any others like that in his parents' circle of friends. So, he pressed the issue, asking, "I have some friends at school who came out this year. Could he be – you know – maybe queer?"

Clive turned ashen. He took a quick sip of wine. "Hmm," Clive murmured. "I don't think so."

"He seems very affectionate with you."

Clive felt himself perspire as Elliott kept posing questions. "He's that way with everyone. It's his Italian demeanor."

Elliott glanced over at Mauro, attending another table. His hands were clasped behind his back as he took the couple's order. Elliott followed him with his eyes, and he interacted with other tables in the same formal way.

"He seems particularly friendly with you. So does Sebastian in the parlor and the guy who stopped by for a brandy yesterday. What was his name?"

"Alex."

"Yes. Alex."

"You're making too much of it. We're all old friends."

"But no one is married, except you."

"Everyone makes choices," Clive said, looking off into the distance.

"How would you know?"

"Know what?"

"If someone is, you know, that way."

"Oh, my lad, that's a complicated question. I don't really know that much about it – not like your generation does."

"Like Mauro, or Sebastian, or Alex – what would be clues if they were homosexual?"

"Hmm," Clive began, wondering how he might frame things to a curious eighteen-year-old struggling to make sense of himself.

"There are the obvious ones whose mannerisms and way of dress give them away."

Elliott nodded. He thought he knew what Clive meant.

"But others are not so easy to identify. I imagine most homosexuals are indistinguishable from anyone else."

Elliott felt blood rush to his face. He hoped he wasn't one.

"Is it a choice?"

Clive shook his head. "No. I don't think so. It's something that seizes you at the core of your being. It's something you can try to resist, but it's always there. It's undeniable."

Entranced and terrified, Elliott leaned forward. "What does it feel like?" he asked, assuming that his wise grandfather had answers, although he never really considered how a heterosexual man would be able to describe the phenomenon. He felt confident Clive had answers and insights.

Trying to frame things as innocently as possible, Clive said, "I have been told it's the things you notice – someone's eyes following yours or lingering over an introduction or greeting. A flutter in the stomach when you meet someone handsome, someone who draws your attention."

Elliott nodded - his eyes wide open.

"You notice smells — pleasant, almost intoxicating smells. Women wear perfume, and some are quite delightful, but men have an earthy scent, an aroma of strength – oak, pepper, sweat."

Elliott took a deep breath, savoring the subtle smells of their table – the roasted fries of his schnitzel and the brandy and peppercorns in Clive's meat sauce. He recalled walking home to the hotel that evening and smelling the lingering fragrance of Max's citrusy cologne. Elliott blushed.

"There's the difference in a man's touch – a warmth and intensity that settles into your body and makes you stir. For heterosexuals, a woman's touch – smooth and gentle – is satisfying. Homosexuals crave a more forceful and penetrating touch, one that is filled with power, intensity, and passion."

"Do you have friends who are homosexual?"

Clive looked off across the room, and he nervously scratched the back of his hand. Images of Hans flooded his mind - his solid body, playful hair, mustache, and penetrating eyes. He felt his heart flutter and his breathing accelerate.

He knew Mauro, Sebastian, Alex and many others were of his persuasion. He envied their independence but feared the precariousness of their lives. He knew others like them in Britain - men who had confided in him, who had sought solace, and some who had taken their lives. He wanted to encourage his grandson, but he needed to protect the fragile secretive existence he had forged.

"Not really," he answered. "Do you?" he followed.

Elliott twitched nervously and replied, "No. Just some classmates who came out. But they aren't friends."

"You never know who is. So, treat everyone will respect and understanding. You never know what someone is going through."

Elliott thought back to Max, the image of his fist clenched at his side and the terrifying look in his eyes. Maybe he was one, or maybe he thought Elliott was one. He felt his heart pound.

He arched his back, pulled back his shoulders, and cocked his head slightly. Although it might be the case that queers were indistinguishable from others, he would at least do his best to look normal. He was normal, he thought to himself. He glanced over at his grandfather, who was so handsome, athletic, and smart. Everyone loved him – a gregarious and larger-than-life kind of person. He had been a good husband and father and grandfather. Elliott benefitted from his generosity and love of travel. Elliott envied his grandfather's cosmopolitan flair – the ease at which he spoke many languages and his comfort with other cultures and ways of life.

Clive looked at his grandson and smiled warmly.

Elliott smiled back. Elliott felt something shift inside. The dueling thoughts about who he was and who he wanted to be seemed to take a pause. He felt a sense of calm and resolve as he gazed at the wise and inspiring man in front of him. Yes. That is who he wanted to be. Yes. That is who he would be.

9

⌘

Chapter Nine – Going Home

Mürren November 1918

A few days later, Clive entered a hall inside the Princess Hotel, where military authorities were coordinating arrangements for the repatriation of prisoners. Clive wore his uniform. He looked handsome and healthy, and he was eager to get on with his life.

"Williams, Clive," the sergeant began.

"Yes, sir," he responded.

"You're part of the Yorkshire regiment, correct?"

"Yes, sir."

"You've been under the care of Doctor Hans Weber, correct?"

"Yes, sir."

"It says in your file that your leg injuries have healed, and your TB was undetectable."

"Yes, sir."

"But there are recent notations that suggest your TB has returned. Doctor Weber is recommending a delay of your repatriation."

Clive didn't respond to the surprising information. He felt blood rush to his face. He stared at a piece of art on the wall to avoid eye contact with the officers.

"Is this true?"

"I don't know, sir. I feel fine. The last time Dr. Weber examined me, everything was clear."

"That doesn't seem to be the case, now," one of the officials at the table noted.

Clive wrestled with whether to challenge the information in his file or not. Raising questions about the records might lead to trouble for them both.

The sergeant then stated, "We don't want to jeopardize your health in sending you home, particularly in the winter and to a country whose resources are depleted."

Clive responded respectfully, "I understand, sir. However, my family has resources, and we have close medical acquaintances who can monitor my symptoms. I'm sure the symptoms are only an anomaly."

The sergeant shook his head and whispered to several of his colleagues. He then turned back toward Clive and said, "We recommend that you remain here in Mürren. However, if you can assure us that you have independent resources at home, we can approve your transfer."

"Thank you, sir. Yes. I can assure you that I will seek medical care and that I have the resources to do so."

The military officials hesitated. They observed Clive. He was tall and fit. He didn't look ill. He looked eager to return home. The sergeant glanced at his colleagues, who nodded. He looked up and declared forcefully, "Approved for transfer."

Clive heard the loud and reassuring sound of a forceful stamp on the documents he would need to return home. The officials handed them to him. Clive saluted the military team and made his exit.

He left the hotel and walked briskly through the village. He was angry. He passed the hotel where he was housed and glanced up at the second floor, at the window of Hans' office. He murmured under his voice, "Hans Weber, go to hell!" Several soldiers passing by looked at him curiously.

He passed a small tavern. Fellow soldiers were spilling out of the tightly packed space, everyone eager to celebrate the end of the war. Several of Clive's comrades waved him in.

"Clive, Clive. Come join us!"

He nodded no.

One of them, Harry, grabbed hold of Clive's arm, saying, "We're leaving tomorrow. You've got to join us."

Clive protested with his eyes, but Harry was tenacious. He held Clive's arm and thread them through the throng up to the bar. "*Zwei Bier, bitte.*"

Harry turned to Clive and said, "When are you heading back?"

"I don't know yet."

Another comrade, Martin, approached and slung his arm over Clive's shoulder. His breath smelled of beer and his voice slurred, "Clive. Haven't seen you around much. Where have you been?"

"Here and there," Clive replied as he took a stein of beer from the bartender and took an evasive sip.

"We'll have to get together when we're back," Harry said excitedly as he raised his stein in a toast to his friends.

Clive nodded, still conflicted about whether to leave Switzerland or not.

Martin pulled a photo from his pocket. He held it out for Harry and Clive to see. "Caroline and I will get married next month."

"Congratulations," Clive said with forced emotion.

"And you?" Martin asked Clive and Harry.

They glanced at each other. Harry knew Clive's secret and nodded to him, as if he understood Clive's pain and confusion.

Harry then said, "I've been writing to a friend of my sister. Her husband died in France. She's eager to meet me."

Martin asked, "What does she look like?"

"My sister says she's beautiful and lively – blonde hair, red cheeks, full bosom."

Clive nodded warmly. Both stared at him, waiting for him to speak of his plans.

"I'm in no hurry to settle down," Clive observed. "I want to check on my parents and look for a job."

More comrades approached, all heavily lubricated with beer. Several showed pictures of their girlfriends and talked excitedly about wedding plans and a new future. Clive was superficially excited for them, expressing congratulations. His comrades were genuinely curious about his plans. Everyone liked him and conveyed their interest in staying in touch.

One friend even said, "Clive, let's plan on a rendezvous here in Mürren to ski. Once we have jobs and things are back to normal, we should all come back."

Everyone nodded enthusiastically. The suggestion startled Clive. Where would he be in a couple of years and, if not in Mürren, could he ever return? Clive began to perspire nervously. He needed air quickly. He finished the beer and excused himself. Outside, he took a path that led out of town toward Allmendhubel. He needed to burn off steam and think. Turning off the main road, he took a path, one that meandered through a thick grove of fir trees and past several barns that sheltered cattle in the winter. He passed familiar landmarks, places he and his fellow soldiers had used for tobogganing, skiing and, in the summer, rugby. He climbed the steep hill. Periodically, he glanced down at the village. It was so beautiful, a pristine Alpine hamlet perched high in the mountains.

He had grown to love the place, and he wanted to remain. But the idea of being Hans' secret liaison bothered him. Everyone else was returning home to get married, form households, start careers. Did he really want to be Hans' hotel manager, who got shagged on the side when Hans got horny? Could he deal with Hans' regret and shame, never to hear the words, 'I love you'? Could he marry just to create the façade of respectability? And to whom? It was all very distressing.

He continued his walk. The more he thought about it, the angrier he became. Over the last year, he kept hoping Hans would come around, would admit his affections, and make peace with himself. He obviously hadn't, and the violation of trust in doctoring his records only reaffirmed the lengths Hans would go to manipulate him.

He climbed to the top of Allmendhubel. He took a deep breath; one he was incapable of taking two years earlier. He was grateful for escaping death on the battlefield, his luck in being sent to Switzerland, and the excellent care he had received while a prisoner. As much as Hans' guilt and shame annoyed him, he had to admit that their relationship had been a blessing. Even in the darkest times of the war, he could count on an escape with Hans – a momentary flight to a place where his body and his desires were one, where he didn't have to fear hostility or reprisal, and where he could have stimulating conversations and warm companionship.

Clive wanted to walk away in protest; return to England to start over again. But things were not so straightforward. England was a conservative country, and he lived in a rural community where everyone knew everyone else's business. It was always difficult to find someone of similar persuasion – much less someone as handsome, smart, and rich as Hans. He felt his heart flutter anxiously, the realization that while Hans' inability to accept their love was frustrating, at least it was a certain thing in a very tumultuous and hostile world.

He glanced at the massive mountains in front of him – solid, timeless, immutable. The mountains had become his friends. He had grown familiar with their groves, ravines, and gullies. When he hiked and skied, they inspired him to dream and imagine.

His head was a swirl of conflicting emotions – anger, resentment, desire, love, affection, disappointment. He felt both idealistic and practical — wanting to challenge and change the world, yet realizing that what Hans offered made practical sense. Would he ever have a similar opportunity in the future? He glanced across the valley at the sunshine reflecting off the snow-covered Jungfrau peak. Should he be uncompromising, taking no less than an unambiguous declaration of love from Hans, or should he settle for a simulacrum of a relationship?

He pressed his hands against his temples, hoping the battle inside would subside. It didn't. He belted out a scream – a forceful release of air and sound – wishing the mountains would echo a reply, would solve his dilemma. There was only silence. No one was there to counsel him or offer a path forward. He realized he was master of his own destiny, the author of his life. For better or for worse, he would have to decide. He would have to choose.

He took a deep breath, going over the pros and cons of each option. His heart fluttered each time he thought of Hans. How could he leave him – relinquish his solid body, his playful smile, and the way his heart raced when Hans stared into his eyes?

But each time he visualized their being together, he couldn't shake the image of Margrit and Conrad sitting beside him in their parlor. Even if Hans thought the arrangement was perfect, Clive realized it cheated him and Margrit of anything approximating authentic love. His conscience disturbed him. It was one thing to succumb to Hans' advances here and there during an unusual time, during a time of war. But to embark on a lifelong arrangement that paralleled Hans' and Margrit's marriage was too morally troubling. He couldn't take that step, certainly not if Hans couldn't even tell him he loved him.

He began to murmur words aloud – words directed to the forest and to the mountains. "Regretfully, I have to leave. You have given me strength and made me feel whole and alive. You have shown me affection – affection I never imagined possible. I will carry you and the memories of Mürren with me forever. *Adieu.*"

Clive felt a pinch in his chest as he murmured the words to himself. He wondered if Hans would feel the same pain he felt now – the ache of two souls torn apart by a cruel world, one that shamed their love and forced unthinkable decisions. He knew he would never get over Hans. He imagined Hans would find another male lover - someone for whom a clandestine relationship was convenient; perhaps someone who loathed himself equally.

A stiff breeze blew through the trees and over the snow-covered ground on which he stood. He pulled the collar of his coat up higher around his neck and crossed his arms in front of his chest. He felt a chill and decided to return to his lodgings and prepare for his return to England.

10

Chapter Ten – The Schilthorn

Mürren Winter 2007

Sofia brought a steaming cup of coffee to Elliott's table and said, "Good morning. How are you doing?"

"Good, thanks."

"I'm so sorry for disturbing you yesterday," Sofia said, furrowing her brows.

"Oh, not a problem. It was fascinating to learn more about the connections of our families."

"Yes, indeed," Sofia said. She felt blood rush to her face, and she tried her best to conceal her dismay at what she had found in Clive's medical file.

Elliott didn't notice Sofia's disquiet and said, "Looks like a beautiful day outside."

"Yes, we received about thirty centimeters of new snow. The conditions should be amazing," Sofia remarked, grateful to focus on more pleasant things.

"I was thinking of going up to Birg and to the Schilthorn."

"Oh!" Sofia exclaimed, alarmed. She wasn't sure Elliott was prepared for the challenges of the upper slopes.

"Is there a problem?" he asked, picking up on Sofia's concern.

"No. No. The conditions should be excellent up there. Are you going alone?"

Elliott looked around his table playfully. "I'm afraid it's just me."

Sofia had a restless night, tossing and turning as she tried to put pieces of a puzzle together – the postcard from Margrit to Clive, Clive's reticence to visit Mürren, and the inexplicable notations in Clive's medical chart at the end of the war. She could only surmise that there must have been affection between Hans and Clive and that Clive must have felt great sadness when he left. Sofia couldn't help thinking that Elliott carried some of his grandfather's grief – an under the surface regret that seemed to show on his face, in his gestures, and in the energy that surrounded him.

She worried about Max. He seemed exceptionally irritable and impatient. Sure, there were the typical stressors of running an inn – the breakdown of equipment, the cost of supplies, the concern about bookings, and the peculiarities of certain guests. Elliott wasn't a difficult guest. In fact, he was quite easy compared to the rambunctious kids that tracked snow into the front entrance, broke furniture in the parlor, and dropped food in the dining room. But Elliott seemed to have pushed some buttons with Max, and Sofia wanted to get to the bottom of it.

"I have an idea. Maybe Max can accompany you today. A few of our guests have left, so we don't have a full house. He needs a break. He's always wanting to get out and ski, and today is the perfect day."

Elliott looked at Sofia incredulously. "Really?"

"Yes," she said, nodding. She looked troubled and not as certain as her words conveyed.

Elliott felt Sofia might be setting a trap, but he was apprehensive about going up to the Schilthorn alone. A local would provide much needed guidance and encouragement. He said, "Well. If it's not too much of a bother, that would be nice. I would feel more confident if someone who knew his way around accompanied me."

"I'll have a chat with Max," she replied.

Sofia retreated to the kitchen. Elliott thought he heard Max and Sofia exchange words, loud words, contentious words. Soon, Max appeared at Elliott's table. He was agitated. He looked back and forth in the dining room, avoiding eye contact with Elliott. He finally faced him and said, "Looks like I'm to accompany you to the upper slopes."

Elliott didn't like Max's tone. He felt like he was now a burden or a chore for the day. He said, "I'm quite alright. I think Sofia is concerned about me. I'll be fine."

Max stared at Elliott and said, "No. We would be horrified if you got into trouble. I'll accompany you. I'm always asking for a ski day. I might as well take one when it's offered."

"When would you like to go up?"

"Well, I could be ready in an hour. We can walk down to the tram station and take the cable car to Birg and then to the Schilthorn. Sound okay?"

Elliott nodded. Max left in a hurry. Elliott finished his coffee, downed a second croissant, and headed upstairs to dress.

An hour later, Max stood at the front door of the inn, dressed for a day on the slopes. He had on a slim pair of dark ski pants and a red ski jacket, a newer model – lightweight and windproof. He held a helmet and goggles in one hand, and his skis and poles in another. "Ready?" he inquired as Elliott approached.

Elliott nodded, uncertain of Max's mood.

Max scrutinized Elliott as he walked out of the front door ahead of him. He had on a dark blue pair of ski pants and a turquoise jacket with new boots and an expensive pair of Swiss skis. He seemed like the quintessential tourist — all decked out with the latest clothes and equipment as if an expert skier but hidden behind the façade was, at best, an adequate intermediate. Max resented Sofia's having put him on the spot to spend the day with Elliott. The conditions were perfect. He could have skied the mountain at liberty, but now feared he would be held back, having to take care of his amateur and pretentious guest.

They walked the short distance to the tram station that would take them to Birg. The silence between them was deafening, broken only by the crunching sound of ski boots on the fresh snow. "Looks like a great day," Elliott remarked, breaking the silence and hoping to elicit some excitement from Max.

Max looked up at the mountains, as if Elliot's observation had been unexpected. He nodded and murmured a timid response, "Hmm. Yes."

"When you ski, do you usually go up to the Schilthorn?" Elliott inquired, trying to get Max to be more talkative.

"It depends on the conditions," Max responded without elaboration.

Elliott realized it was going to be a tortuous day, given Max's reticence to engage in conversation.

They approached the station, walked inside, and waited for the cable car from the valley to arrive. As it did, countless passengers disembarked and made their way to the next car, going higher. Max gestured for them to join the throng, and they found a space near the front window.

Max slipped on a pair of sunglasses and gazed out of the window – silent and inscrutable. Elliott didn't know if he was shy or annoyed.

The cable car lifted out of the station and began to float in the air. The terrain rose sharply, almost vertically, below them. The cable car rocked gently as it rose. Elliott had a fear of heights. Although he was an avid skier, he avoided lifts that were too high or perched on vulnerable terrain. He felt his palms sweat. He looked out onto the distant horizon, hoping that might calm his nerves.

Max gazed out of the window at the town of Mürren, receding from view. The Traumblick was a small speck at the edge of the village. He felt guilty leaving Sofia at home to do the chores. She kept insisting that he go despite his protests. He wondered why.

Several local men stood nearby. Max listened in as they made comments about the fresh snow. They nodded to him. He greeted them warmly, saying, "*Hallo mitenand. Schöne Tag.*"

Ever since his first trip to Grindelwald, Elliott wanted to belong to the handsome men his grandfather greeted in their local dialect. He worked tirelessly to learn their language, hoping it might be his entrée. He had grown to appreciate as a gay man that his love for languages was, in some way, an acknowledgement of other worlds. Being gay, he lived in a parallel world. Gaining entry into another felt transgressive, in an exciting sort of way. He gazed at Max and his local acquaintances. They were tall and muscular and carried their skis like totems - long, hard, erect shafts of wood and steel.

Elliott envied their tribe. He wanted in; he wanted to be accepted, to belong. He tried to catch their attention with a glance, a raised brow, a smile. They seemed elusive, almost as if they knew he wanted their attention and response, and they weren't going to give it. Max was the weak link, the place where he might breach their defenses. Strategically, Elliott drew on his best language skills and asked Max where they were headed, "*Wohin gehen wir?*"

Max sighed and lifted one hand and pointed up. Elliott wondered if Max sniffed out his motive and gave him a half-hearted response or was embarrassed and hoped not to draw attention to the two of them.

Elliott saw nothing but rock. He returned a quizzical look.

Max added, "*Die andere Seite. Da oben.*"

"Ah," Elliott replied, realizing there was more terrain just higher up on the other side of the ridge. Max was reserved, sharing as little information as possible.

As the cable car rose, bright sunshine filled the cabin. Max's face became luminous. He remained stoic and evasive, staring straight ahead. Elliott's feet became cold, and his palms perspired as the car dangled precariously in midair. Elliott resented how calm and self-assured Max appeared.

They arrived at Birg and changed for the car that would carry them even higher. Elliott wondered if that was a mistake. He was already terrified at the height they had climbed. He asked, "*Wollen wir hier skifahren?*"

Max nodded no, gesturing for them to walk toward the next car. Elliott followed, trembling inside. As they pressed against the window, and Elliott glanced down at the steep drop-off, he thought he detected a cruel grin on Max's face.

They continued the ascent. Max pointed out a couple of runs they would take later. Soon, they arrived at the terminus and walked into the complex. Many exiting the cable car were tourists hoping to enjoy the panoramic views of the Alps and have lunch in the restaurant. A small contingent of hard-core skiers with serious equipment and clothing made their way outside.

"This is where James Bond skied, right?" Elliott asked, certain as he formulated the question that Max would be mortified and embarrassed by his tourist companion.

"Yes," Max said, rolling his eyes when Elliott wasn't looking. "Let's go," he added impatiently.

They exited the building to a sunny flat area where skiers put on their skis and prepared for the descent. Max quickly stepped into his bindings and peered down the mountain. It was a challenging run, even for locals. "You know, if one skied all the way to Lauterbrunnen, it would be a jaw dropping seven thousand foot vertical," he remarked, proud of the massive mountain he called home.

"You're kidding!" Elliott said, his brows raised and his mouth open. "Are we doing all of that?"

"No. We'll ski here on the upper slopes, and at the end of the day, head down to Mürren. There are some nice gentle trails to end our excursion. Going all the way to Lauterbrunnen isn't that interesting, even if the vertical difference is impressive. The vertical to Mürren is over 4000 feet. That should be good enough!"

Elliott sighed in relief. He glanced over at Max, who was making last-minute adjustments to his boots, helmet, and gloves. "*Heute ist ein schöner Tag*," Max began as he leaned up, pointing his ski pole down the slope in front of them. "The first part is steep but, when the snow is fresh and the sun is out like today, it is soft, and your skis will grip nicely."

Elliott nodded nervously. He was a good skier. His grandfather had taught him well and had taken him down other challenging runs in the region. He wanted to impress Max and hoped he would be in good form. He looked down the slope. It was steep and the left side of the trail looked like it was a sheer vertical drop to a ledge at least a thousand feet below. He wasn't worried so much about the trail. It was the side of it that bothered him.

They pushed off the prep area and began to glide on the packed powder surface. Max led. He made several well placed and controlled turns. Elliott followed suit. They continued down the slope. It was steep, but as Max had promised, the skis gripped the surface nicely.

Suddenly, Max yelled, "*Scheisse!*"

"What?" Elliott yelled back to him in alarm.

Max skidded to a stop, and Elliott stopped right behind him.

"Look there. The wind has blown all the fresh snow off. It's all ice below here."

Elliott watched as a couple of expert skiers edge into the icy surface. They made their turns but ended up skidding many meters before being able to grip the surface enough to make the next turn.

Max surveyed the slope. On the left side of the run, the side where there was a sheer drop, the safety nets and banks of snow had protected a small path from the wind. "We can go over there and catch some good snow until we get farther down the slope, where the wind doesn't hit the trail."

Elliott felt his hands sweat and his legs tense up. He traversed to the left, following Max. As he got to the edge of the trail, the edge that was in better condition, he glanced over the side and couldn't see the bottom. It was his greatest nightmare.

Max noticed Elliott tensing up. "We can take it easy. Just make short turns here in the good snow."

Elliott couldn't move. Frozen in place, he feared if he began to glide forward, his legs wouldn't turn, and he would head straight for the ice. If he hugged the side of the trail near the safety net, he imagined crashing through it and falling to his death. He began to tremble.

Max realized Elliott was in trouble. He took careful steps on the steep slope toward him. When he stood near him, he asked, "Are you okay?"

"No!" Elliott exclaimed without elaboration.

"We can take it slow and easy."

Elliott didn't respond.

Max mumbled to himself, "I knew this was going to be a mistake."

Elliott could feel Max's frustration and irritation. "Why don't you ski down? I'll take my time and catch up to you."

Max wanted to do just that, but a voice in his head said, "Stay with him."

Max inched closer to Elliott. He peered down the run, wondering if there might be another route to take. Even he was apprehensive of the glaze of ice on their right and the narrow band of snow on the left, now being skied on by others coming down the trail.

Elliott watched the experts race past them, making short quick turns. Several skidded on the underlying slick surface despite their skill.

Max inched closer toward Elliott to get out of the way of those barreling down the piste. As he did, Elliott tensed up and screamed, "Don't push me!"

Max lifted his hands and said, "Don't worry. I won't." He looked into Elliott's eyes. They were filled with terror. He continued, "Why don't we side slip as far as we can? We can see how far we get doing that and, when the surface gets better, we can ski the rest of the way down."

Max began a few controlled slides, and Elliott followed. His legs were weak and tense, but he managed to remain standing.

Expert skiers raced past them. More and more got into trouble as the fresh snow was skied off. Elliott felt vindicated. He wasn't the only one having difficulty.

Eventually, they arrived at an area where the wind had not blown the snow away. The trail was soft, and the conditions ideal. They stopped.

"Oh my God," Elliott remarked, his heart pounding with adrenaline. "I'm so sorry. I'm so embarrassed."

"Don't be," Max said unconvincingly. "The ice was unexpected."

"I know. But I froze."

"Don't like heights?"

Elliott nodded no.

"But you like to ski."

"A bit confusing, right?"

Max nodded and chuckled slightly. It was the first smile of the day. "Are you okay?"

"Yes. This looks fine. I just have to recompose myself. Let's continue," Elliott said.

Max pushed off and began to make beautiful turns on the trail. Elliott followed. At the beginning, his legs were tense, but he made a few good turns and felt his rhythm return.

Max stopped down the hill, lifted his goggles, and looked up. Elliott was making graceful turns, very controlled turns. In fact, he was stunned. Elliott looked like he could be a ski instructor. He had perfect form. Elliott skied up to Max and skidded to a stop.

"I'm dumbfounded," Max remarked, shaking his head.

Elliott peered into Max's hazel eyes. They sparkled in the bright light reflecting off the snow. He was smiling broadly, small dimples forming on the side of his mouth. Max continued, "Where did you learn to ski?"

"That bad, huh?"

"No. I'm amazed. At the top, I had my doubts. But what I just saw is nothing short of astounding. Beautiful form, perfect control, nice agility. Where did you pick that up? I only see that in the best skiers here."

"My grandfather," Elliott replied, delighted that he had breached Max's hard shell at last.

"Oh yes, Sofia mentioned something about him. Seems there is a connection between our families dating back to the First World War."

"My grandfather was a prisoner in Mürren. Hans was a doctor and took care of him."

"And you ended up at the Traumblick," Max said with a hint of sarcasm. Despite Elliott's newly revealed skiing ability, Max still considered him annoying and odd.

"Yes. There was a postcard from here with the hotel's name."

"Hmm," Max murmured. "So, your grandfather learned to ski here, on these slopes?"

"Hm hmm," Elliott remarked, gazing out at the beautiful horizon. "He learned when modern skiing was just getting started."

Max nodded and smiled, but he was restless. The clock was ticking, and they had only skied a fraction of the terrain. "Shall we ski down to the next lift?"

Elliott nodded. Max pushed off and skied aggressively down the mountain. When he arrived at the bottom of the run, to his surprise, Elliott was right behind him. They lined up for the chairlift. Once seated, they lowered the safety bar and headed up.

With time to kill on the lift, Max was slightly more talkative and asked, "So, you said you learned how to ski from your grandfather? He must have been quite good."

"He skied until his mid-80s. When I was a teenager, he took me on ski trips to the Alps – often to Grindelwald."

"He skied that long?"

"Yes," Elliott said proudly.

Max tried to imagine Elliott learning to ski as a teenager with his grandfather. Had he been lanky and awkward, or athletic and handsome? He glanced over and looked at Elliott's legs. They were muscular. He pretended to adjust his gloves and pole, leaning back a little. He took a quick stealth look at Elliott's torso – long, lean, and powerful. As he did so, he had an odd sensation, as if he had met Elliott before. Since their inn catered to Brits, he had met many over the years, but there was something eerily familiar about Elliott that he couldn't quite put his finger on.

Out of curiosity, he asked, "But you never skied in Mürren? I'm surprised, given your grandfather's time here."

"I think it was too painful." Elliott glanced over at Max, who was staring off to the right at a slope under the lift. He glanced furtively at his face. It was flush from their run down. A dark, short-cropped beard circled his mouth and lined his jaw. He had a long, beautiful nose and high cheekbones. He was handsome. Suddenly Max turned and peered into Elliott's eyes. They both held their gaze for a protracted moment, just long enough to realize their antipathy was melting and both were curious about the other.

Earlier, Elliott feared he had lost Max's esteem during his panic attack. It was what haunted him most - showing terror, insecurity, vulnerability. His grandfather had been a commanding and self-assured individual. His own father had been demanding and severe. Over the years, Elliott felt like he had let them both down; that he had been a failure. Although he was professionally successful, his personal life was a mess. He had divorced and gone through a string of failed relationships, only to come to terms with his sexual orientation in the end.

When he came out, his grandfather had been understanding, even gleeful. He wondered if he hadn't taken delight in how the news disturbed his son, Elliott's father, who was all about appearances. Elliott always wondered if his grandfather was an ally, perhaps sharing his proclivities, but he never self-identified as gay. Elliott's parents tolerated him and his boyfriends, his mother reminding him that she would have liked grandchildren. Now that his parents and grandparents had passed, he felt untethered.

Elliott noticed Max seemed more relaxed. He cocked his head back and let the sun caress his face. As he did, Elliott sighed. For some reason, he felt responsible for Max's comfort, even though it was Max who was looking after him. He thought it a peculiar sensation.

Suddenly, Max asked, "Is your father still alive?"

"No. My parents have both passed. But why do you ask?"

"I don't know. I guess I was wondering if skiing was in your family's blood. Did your father ski, too?"

"A little, but he and my mother were not that into winter sports. What about yours?"

"Both have passed, as well. They had a difficult life, running the inn without much help. But my father felt it was important for me to learn to ski. I took lessons early. When the season began to wind down, we would all ski together. It was nice."

"So, the inn has been in the family for a while?"

"Yes. Hans bought it just after the First World War."

"Hmm," Elliott murmured. "Wasn't he a doctor?"

"Yes. He ended up doing both – maintaining a medical practice and running the inn."

Elliott furrowed his brow. It didn't make sense. He wondered if there wasn't a backstory. "Why?" he asked.

Max lifted his hands and said, "I have no idea. It's a good question."

"So, back to your grandfather," Max continued, changing subjects. "That's amazing that he was skiing so late in life."

"He was quite the athlete."

"And you used to ski with him?"

"Every chance I could!"

Max smiled at Elliott, reassessing his earlier judgements. Could Elliott be a bit more interesting than he had imagined? Had he been too hasty in his dismissal of him?

They arrived at the top of the lift and skied down to another lift, farther down the mountain. The views of the slopes and surrounding peaks were breathtaking. They stopped from time to time to take in the scenery and catch their breath. Max skied aggressively. Elliott kept up. Both seemed keen to prove their skills and stamina.

After several runs, Max asked, "Are you hungry? There's a nice, simple place up here where we can get something to eat and take a break."

Elliott nodded. They skied farther down and approached a wood structure with enviable views of the surrounding Jungfrau region. People had begun to take their places in chaises to take in the midday sun and drink cold beer. "*Sieht es gut aus?*" Max asked if the place looked alright.

Elliott wasn't sure if the switch to German was a way to avoid looking like a tourist or perhaps a small gesture of hospitality, a way of letting Elliott in, even if only slightly.

"*Es ist perfekt. Ich lade dich ein,*" Elliott offered to pay.

Max nodded toward a table that was free, and they walked over. They took seats, and a server approached and took their orders.

"Thanks for showing me around," Elliott began as Max fussed with his helmet and goggles and placed them securely under his seat. "I hope I'm not holding you back."

"*Nein. Du bist ein guter Skifahrer,*" Max said politely. He would have preferred a day alone, one unencumbered by a guest. But, as the day progressed, he felt less resentful and enjoyed having someone to talk to as they rode the lifts. He added, now in English, "Aside from the first part of the run at the top, you're formidable. I'm impressed."

"After my clumsy incident the other morning, you probably had me pegged as a certifiable sissy from Britain."

Max grinned. "Well, you put on a good act!"

The server returned with two beers and a stew made of some local mountain goat and winter vegetables. Elliott lifted his glass to Max's and said, "Cheers! To a great day on the slopes."

"To the best English skier I've ever met!" Max replied, raising his glass.

Elliott choked on the gulp of beer he had just taken, shocked at Max's gregarious remark. He coughed a couple of times, cleared his throat, and said, "Flattery will get you a good review of the inn, Mr. Weber."

"You promise?"

They both chuckled.

Elliott looked evasively away from Max, not sure how to process his adulation. Max perceived Elliott's incredulity and said, "Really. I didn't expect it."

"I'm full of surprises," Elliott remarked, wishing he had perhaps toned his banter down. He didn't want Max to retreat into his defensive shell, nor did he want him to discover his real secrets - his desires, fantasies, cravings.

"The other night you said you didn't have children yet. I notice you don't have a ring. You're single?"

Oh shit, Elliott thought to himself. He hadn't expected Max to start asking personal questions. He had been so inscrutable and aloof before, and he wondered if that wasn't better. "Divorced," he replied without elaboration.

"Hmm," Max murmured. "Contentious?"

"Not really. We were young. We didn't know what we were doing. It's for the best."

"Any romantic interests?"

Elliott felt flush. He enjoyed Max's curiosity. It signified that a handsome man had found him intriguing and wanted to get to know him. But it was a two-edged sword, particularly if the handsome man was straight and began to uncover Elliott's under-the-surface inclinations.

"Not really," Elliott replied nonchalantly, hoping Max wouldn't pry further.

"Thus, the reason for your coming to a wild singles ski resort!" Max joked.

"Exactly," Elliott replied. He took a bite of the stew and washed it down with a swig of beer. He thought hard about how he could steer the conversation away from his personal life. He said, "In reality, I was curious why my grandfather was reluctant to come to Mürren when we used to ski in Grindelwald. I always thought it was strange, inexplicable. I presumed he left broken-hearted. When I saw your great grandmother's signature on the postcard, 'love Margrit,' it only seemed to confirm as much. I guess I wanted to visit the town that had been so impactful in his life."

"But, from what Sofia said, Margrit was only letting your grandfather know that Hans had died, presumably because Hans had taken care of him during the war."

Sofia had already shared what she had found in the archives with Max, that Hans seemed to have had a deep affection for Elliott's grandfather and tried to prevent his return home. She was mortified and hoped Elliott wouldn't uncover the truth. Max tried to frame the correspondence in the most innocent way possible, but he wondered if he wasn't falling under the spell of Clive's grandson, if history wasn't repeating itself. He glanced over at Elliott. He wanted to dislike him, resent him, despise him. But he had those damn, haunting, deep brown, alluring eyes. Elliott was fastidious and a control freak. He was oblivious – a single man booking a ski vacation at a family-oriented resort. But, despite the annoying things, Elliott had proven to be quite the athlete, was handsome, and easy to talk to. He then began to imagine the unimaginable. His body trembled as frightful and shameful fantasies swirled in his head. What would it be like to touch him, to feel his skin against his own, and to take hold of what he imagined must be an impressive package inside his tight ski pants?

He shook his head to dispel the desires. He adjusted his sunglasses and stiffened, putting back in place the shield he had dropped earlier in the day. The moment would have been the right one to have a conversation with Elliott about Clive and Hans, to have a conversation about what kind of friends Hans and Clive might have become, and what adventures they may have shared during the war. But he couldn't. It was too close to home, too frightening, too painful.

Max reinforced the story line he hoped Elliott would buy. "I'm sure there were a lot of soldiers who were grateful for the care they received here. Some must have kept in touch. I'm sure your grandfather was well-liked, remarkable, someone Hans would have looked after."

They both let the topic drop. It was a minefield neither was ready to cross. They finished the stew and ordered another round of beers.

Elliott relished the unobstructed views of the mountains. The Eiger, Mönch, and Jungfrau loomed in the distance, partially concealed in a bluish haze. The landscape was both breathtaking and ominous. The magnitude and ethereal nature of the peaks suggested a hidden world of gods and goddesses, divine beings who spied on mortals and arranged their destinies. Elliott sensed there was a purpose in his being there; that destiny had brought the grandson and great grandson of Hans and Clive together. Their meeting was too laden with significance to be an accident. They were skiing where Clive first learned to ski, and Elliott was a guest in the lodge Hans bought. The coincidences were too compelling to be accidental.

They both sat quietly with their thoughts. Both sensed that Hans and Clive were present – smiling and nudging them toward one another. Both feared what that meant.

Max pierced the silence and said, "Shall we continue? It's time to make our way back down to the village. There's a route here below that winds down to a narrow trail leading to Allmendhubel where we can take any number of runs back home."

"You said a narrow trail?" Elliott asked, jolted back to the reality of the challenging mountain before them. He wasn't sure what frightened him more – the challenging ski trails or the uncertain terrain opening between him and Max.

"It's not that narrow or steep. Given what you traversed earlier, you can handle whatever the mountain throws at you!"

Elliott wasn't convinced. He glared at Max and felt his legs grow weak.

They paid their tab, retrieved their skis, and began to make their way down the mountain. They took an expert slope below the lifts, one that curved gently toward a longer trail that crossed a deep valley. They stopped and surveyed the terrain.

"You said it wasn't that daunting," Elliott remarked with consternation, realizing there was no alternative route.

"I've seen you ski. There's nothing you can't handle."

"Heights."

"Just stay focused on what is in front of you. Don't look to the side."

Elliott pushed off and advanced along the trail. He felt his legs tense up as he glanced at the steep drop off at the side of the run. He wasn't skiing confidently, and he feared he would trip at any moment.

"Keep looking forward," Max yelled at him.

"Fuck looking forward," Elliott murmured to himself, irritated that Max had led him there. He glanced again at the dramatic plunge of terrain just feet away. The piste was only slightly inclined, but that didn't matter. He was convinced he would trip and tumble down the rocky precipice.

A few skiers flew past him, some of them young teens. He saw Max waiting for him at the end of the trail. He wanted to impress him. He wanted to impress himself. Was he willing to let go of his fear and simply look forward? He took a deep breath and concentrated on the words of his grandfather echoing in his head. "Keep your body facing down the hill, no matter how frightening it seems. As counterintuitive as it may seem, facing the incline, facing the steepness before you, is the only way you will be in control."

He peered forward and made several graceful turns. A few moments later, he skied up to Max.

"Bravo! I knew you could do it."

Elliott wanted to yell at Max for putting him in such a frightful situation, but he held back and smiled. He leaned on his poles and took a deep breath. It was a good feeling.

Max then nudged him playfully with his pole and said, "Now it's just a few easy trails to the inn. Race you?"

Elliott didn't nod or acknowledge Max's dare. He used his powerful legs to skate with his skis and pushed off in a flash. Max yelled, "*Scheisse*," and leaned forward, using his poles to initiate his own descent just behind Elliott.

They crouched low to the ground and took the curvy trail into the village, dodging families and kids on the way down. Elliott caught a ski edge on one of the turns and flew into a bank of snow. Max skidded to a stop and began to laugh.

Elliott was buried in the deep snow. He unfastened his bindings and began to trudge toward the piste. As he got closer to the edge of the trail, Max extended his pole. Elliott grabbed it and yanked hard. Max lost balance and fell into the snow, too. A skier slowed at the edge of the run and asked, "Are you both okay?"

Max raised his hand as if to say they were fine. The man skied off. As Max turned back toward Elliott, Elliott tossed a snowball in his direction. It landed right on Max's head. Max formed a ball and tossed it at Elliott. Elliott raised his hands and said, "Truce!"

Max raised his and nodded.

They climbed out of the deep snow, brushed themselves off as best they could, and skied to the inn. Sofia was in the front foyer and saw them arrive. She glanced out and furrowed her forehead. She opened the door and said, "What happened to the two of you?"

Max laughed. "Elliott had a little accident with a snowbank. That's all."

Sofia didn't look amused. Max and Elliott were having too much fun, and she needed Max to clean up and get ready to serve dinner later. She glared at him.

Max got the message. He brushed himself clean, shook Elliott's hand, and went inside.

Elliott returned to his room. His legs ached. He began filling the tub with hot water. He took off his ski clothes and slipped into the silky warm water. "Ahh," he said, recalling his adventures with Max.

His phone rang, and Elliott noticed it was Marni. "Marni, how are you doing?"

"The more important question is, how are you doing? The last time we spoke, you feared you had made a big mistake going to Mürren."

"It's still a ski kindergarten here at the hotel, and I'm the odd man out. But I've made friends with the innkeepers."

"Wasn't the husband hot?"

"No, those were the daddies from England and Germany, but yes, he's quite handsome, too."

"Do you need a chaperone?"

Elliott didn't answer.

Marni added, "You're awfully quiet. What's up?"

"He's growing on me. And there are some odd coincidences. His great grandfather and my grandfather were here in this town during the First World War. There was some kind of relationship between them, and I'm beginning to think it could have been romantic."

"Well, that's interesting! Starr-crossed lovers reconnecting through their descendants."

"I'm not sure I would frame it that way, but let's say it wouldn't be surprising if something unfolded. I feel a connection for some odd reason."

"But isn't he married?"

"Minor detail."

"Not really!"

"Yes. You're right. That's a problem," Elliott admitted.

"Promise me you will behave. We don't need to extract a cadaver from the Alps after an angry wife takes her revenge."

"I will. I'm not going to pursue anything. It's just nice to be noticed, to be desired."

"How much longer are you there?"

"Another ten days."

"That's a long ski vacation. How are your legs?"

"Soaking in a tub!"

"Oh! Sorry to have disturbed you. Enjoy."

"Thanks, Marni. Hugs and kisses!"

Marni air kissed Elliott over the phone, and they hung up.

11

Chapter Eleven – The Handsome Prisoner

Mürren Spring 1917

Hans strolled along the sunny terrace of the Princess Hotel. British soldiers reclined on chaises in various stages of undress. Most wore little more than undershorts. Sun beamed onto the south-facing deck. Before the war, the hotel attracted tuberculosis patients who came for heliotherapy. They hoped the crisp dry mountain air and the strong sunshine would dry up the disease.

Recently, the Swiss government had negotiated with foreign governments to house war prisoners in tourist hotels. For foreign countries, it alleviated the burden of maintaining camps, and for the Swiss, it was a safety net for the fragile tourist industry that suffered during the war.

Hans transferred from Bern to Mürren to serve as physician for the internees. Hans found the work both exhilarating and frightening. He glanced down at the row of patients, dozens of young male nude torsos ready for examination. He listened to their breathing, checked their vitals, and probed them for lesions and other ailments. Most were not that attractive, having awful injuries – severed limbs, bullet wounds, and massive scars. Many had lost weight and muscle mass. Despite all of that, Hans found himself fighting urges, alarming ones.

There were some who were in relatively good shape. Their injuries were minor, and their TB was mild. They responded well to exercise, and after weeks in the sun, became tan and fit. There was one, in particular, who stood out, who grabbed his attention.

Clive was tall and robust, with broad shoulders, strong arms, and an enviable chest covered in soft, dark hair. He had black wavy hair and deep brown eyes. He read a lot and always had a warm smile when Hans approached to check his vitals.

Hans and Clive would exchange pleasantries. Hans made it a point to ask what Clive was reading, which led to protracted discussions about art, history, and politics.

Clive found Hans intriguing. He felt the intensity of Hans' eyes and the warmth of his hands as he examined him. Hans easily blushed when he accidentally grazed the side of Clive's pecs or pressed too close to his penis. Clive wondered if Hans didn't share his inclinations.

With time, Clive became bolder. He draped the sheets over himself in more and more provocative ways, and he noticed Hans had a more difficult time concentrating on his work. Clive had always been mischievous. One day, as Hans leaned over his bed, Clive said, "Doctor feel me up, how am I today?"

Hans turned bright red, glanced up and down the row of patients, hoping no one had heard what Clive said, and replied, "Private Williams, you are doing fine. Have a nice day." Hans continued to the next patient in haste.

The next day, Clive repeated the phrase, "Doctor feel me up, how am I?"

Hans shook his head, blushed, and made quick notations on his clipboard. He didn't look Clive in the eyes.

Over the next couple of weeks, Clive continued to use the phrase. Hans was at first embarrassed and nervous but, with time, grew to appreciate the levity during such horrible times. He began to wink at Clive, pat him playfully on the inside of his legs, and grin as he approached in anticipation of Clive's banter.

One day, Clive said, "Doctor feel me up, how am I doing to-day?"

Hans paused, looked Clive in the eyes, and replied, "Is that a declarative or imperative statement?"

Clive returned a quizzical look, surprised at his response.

Hans pressed his stethoscope on Clive's chest and leaned toward him. He whispered, "If it is declarative, it is insolent. You are speaking to a professional, and you should call me Doctor Weber."

"And if it is imperative?" Clive asked with raised brows.

Hans cleared his throat, glanced up and down the row of other patients and whispered, "Well, I can't touch you without your permission," he said, smiling nervously.

Clive raised his hand, gave Hans a salute, and said, "Permission granted."

Hans turned red, scribbled something on his clipboard, and raced off in an uneasy huff.

Clive chuckled. He knew Hans was smitten; that they shared an affinity, and with time, they might enjoy each other more.

The next day, Clive waited for Hans to pass by his bed. Hans avoided eye contact, made notations, and began to take vitals. Clive leaned forward and whispered in Hans' ear, "Doctor, I'm embarrassed. I have a pain in my groin."

Hans stood erect and with a very stoic demeanor said, "Well, that's not my department."

"But doc," Clive implored, "who else is going to examine me? You're the only one taking care of us."

Hans looked off evasively, then turned to Clive and said, "Meet me in my office in an hour."

Later, Clive put on his shirt and trousers and made his way to Hans' office. He knocked on the door, and Hans invited him in. Hans was sweating, smoking, and shuffling papers nervously on his desk. He didn't look Clive in the eyes.

"So, Private Williams, what seems to be the matter?"

Clive realized he had probably pushed Hans too far, and he didn't want to get into trouble. "I'm sorry to disturb you, doc. I think it is a mistake. I'm okay."

Hans looked up and said, "You said you have a pain in your groin. Let's take a look. Let me check your chest first."

Hans came out from behind the desk and approached Clive, who unbuttoned his shirt. Hans gasped for air. Clive was magnificent and, in the intimacy of the office, Hans felt unnerved at the handsome man standing so close to him. He slid his hand inside the folds of the fabric and nuzzled the stethoscope onto Clive's muscular pecs. He slid the stethoscope across Clive's warm skin, grazing his muscles with the side of his hand. He felt himself stir.

"And your groin?"

Clive unbuttoned his trousers and Hans reached his hand inside the undershorts. He began to probe around the side of Clive's sex. It was warm. As he grazed the sides of it, Clive became aroused. Hans' eyes widened, and his heart began to race. He didn't know whether to extract his hand, potentially embarrassing the patient, or continue to examine him as if nothing was out of the ordinary. For a complete exam, he would need to feel around his scrotum and between his legs, and he could only imagine that things would become even more awkward.

Hans glanced up to see how Clive was doing. Their faces were only inches apart, and Hans could feel the warmth of Clive's breath on his face. He fought the urge to take his balls in his hands. He peered into Clive's dark brown eyes, and he felt his legs grow weak. He hesitated and then, suddenly, leaned forward and gave Clive a forceful kiss.

Clive felt Hans' hand moving slowly inside his shorts, and he felt his heart pound as he contemplated what he wanted, what he craved. He kissed Hans back, surrounding Hans' luscious lips with his warm, wet mouth.

Hans closed his eyes at first. Clive thought he heard him moan. But suddenly, Hans stiffened and pulled his hand out of Clive's shorts. He said, "Everything is working fine."

Clive chuckled.

Hans wasn't amused. He returned to his desk and said, "That's all, Private Williams. You have nothing to worry about."

Clive buttoned his shirt and trousers and returned to his bunk.

Over the course of the next couple of weeks, Hans was distant, cold, and professional. He made his rounds and avoided eye contact with Clive. Clive feared he had pushed too far. What he didn't realize was that Hans feared Clive would report him, and he would be sent back to Bern or lose his license.

As time passed, Hans realized Clive hadn't tried to trap him. He relaxed more around Clive and returned to his old self, asking about what Clive was reading and exchanging warm smiles as he cared for his handsome patient.

After Hans returned to his old self, Clive became bolder. "Doctor. I feel a pain here," he said, pointing to his side.

Hans furrowed his brow, looked up and down the row of patients, and placed his warm hand on Clive's side. He probed it tenderly and looked at Clive. "Where does it hurt?"

"Just a little lower," Clive said.

Hans slid his hand farther down Clive's hip, his fingers pressing under his shorts. "Here?"

Clive turned, and Hans' hand grazed his stiffening cock.

Hans turned red, but he didn't retract his hand. Instead, he rubbed his fingers over Clive's sex.

Clive looked into Hans' eyes. Hans looked evasively off into the distance. He said, "I need to do a more careful examination. Can you come to my office later?"

Clive nodded.

An hour later, Clive knocked on Hans' office door. Hans stood up, opened the door, let Clive in, and then closed the door, locking it behind them. He pivoted toward Clive and gazed into his dark, alluring eyes. He felt his legs grow weak.

"So, did you want to take a closer look?" Clive asked, raising his brow.

Hans nodded quietly, his heart racing.

Clive unbuttoned his trousers. They fell to the floor. There was a bulge in his cotton undershorts. Hans reached his warm hand up under Clive's shirt and felt the edges of his pecs, running his fingers through the soft hair covering his chest. He ran his hand down Clive's side. "It was here you were feeling something, right?"

"I think a little lower," Clive said in a soft, trembling voice.

Hans ran his hand down Clive's side and nudged his shorts lower down his hips. Hans felt his heart pound and his body tremble. He looked into Clive's eyes as if to ask permission. They were full of longing.

Hans reached his hand inside Clive's shorts and took hold of him. He began to glide his hand up and down Clive's arousal. With his other hand, Hans took hold of Clive's hand and pressed it onto the front of his trousers, guiding Clive's hands up and down over himself.

Clive wanted to kiss Hans, to feel the moistness of his lips and to breathe him in. He leaned toward him, but Hans turned to the side evasively. He was focused on the flesh in his hand - at its warmth, its thickness, its power.

Clive felt Hans' erection under his own hand. He pressed against the wool trousers and massaged them. Even through the fabric, he could feel Hans' desire growing hard.

Hans squeezed Clive more tightly, running his fingers from the bottom of his shaft to its sensitive end. Hans observed Clive close his eyes. He moaned and cocked his head back as Hans stroked him forcibly. Suddenly, Clive felt waves of pleasure course through his body, and he exploded in spasms of intense delight.

Under his hands, Clive felt Hans' erection stiffen more. Hans edged his pelvis toward Clive. He closed his eyes and allowed himself to ride the mounting force within. Even through the fabric, he felt Clive's large, warm hands. He could feel himself become moist. Thoughts of his life raced through his head – his work, the internees, his wife, his son. The war was demoralizing, and life was hard. For the moment, he relished escaping into the hands of this striking Englishman. He felt handsome and alive and soon felt powerful sensations rise from his legs and explode inside his trousers.

Hans took several deep breaths, and soon his pounding heart returned to normal. He let go of Clive and turned away from him, walking toward the desk. He fussed nervously with some papers. "I think the exam is over," he said matter-of-factly, without warmth or eye contact.

Clive raised his brows, not sure why the sudden change in demeanor. He reached down and pulled up his trousers, tucked in his shirt, and buttoned up. He walked toward Hans. "Doctor. Thank you."

Hans continued to face his desk, away from Clive. He murmured, "Hmm."

Clive made one more attempt, saying, "Doctor?"

Hans said nothing. He continued to look away. Clive thought he heard him say in a soft voice, "Sorry."

Clive left the office and returned to his room.

The next day, during rounds, Hans was his typical jovial self with the other patients. With Clive he was superficially warm, friendly, professional – but, under the surface, Clive detected a reserve.

A week later, during rounds, Hans said to Clive, "Private Williams. Can you come to my office later this afternoon? I want to review some records with you."

Clive nodded.

After lunch, he strolled to Hans' office, knocked, and let himself in. Hans stood, walked to the door, and locked it. "Come have a seat," he gestured to a chair.

Clive took his seat, his heart beating strongly. Hans sat next to him and picked up a file from a small table. He slid his chair near Clive's and said, "I wanted to show you the results of several tests."

Clive looked into Hans' handsome eyes. They sparkled in the orange glow of the embers in the fireplace. Hans leaned toward Clive and placed his elbow between his legs, holding the file for him to see.

Clive raised his brows at the feel of Hans' arms between his legs. After a week of reserve and distance, the casual intimacy was unexpected, even if welcomed.

"You are making exceptional progress in your recovery, Private Williams," Hans said, staring at the file.

"Call me Clive."

Hans pressed his elbow into Clive's formidable inner legs, moving the file back and forth in his hand.

Clive breathed in the pleasant scent of Hans' cologne and felt heat emanate from his body, pressed close to his. Hans' leg was pushed up against his. Clive could feel his own sex stir at the closeness of their bodies.

"See these results?" Hans said, pointing to some numbers.

Clive turned toward Hans. He didn't look at the file. He scrutinized Hans' face. It had become flush. He had trimmed his mustache, making his lips look even more luscious. His eyes were deep, his lashes moist.

Hans realized Clive wasn't looking at the file and turned toward him. Their eyes met. Hans leaned over and gave Clive a long, moist kiss. He dropped the file.

Clive glanced down and noticed Hans was aroused. Clive placed his hands over the erection and watched Hans close his eyes and moan. He slowly began to unbutton Hans' trousers, fearful that at some point, he would object and become dismissive.

He didn't. He leaned back in his chair and let Clive reach in and take hold of him. Clive's hands were smooth and warm and slid up and down Hans' supple, warm flesh. For years, Hans had fought errant desires – first for his comrades at school and later for the occasional patient who had dreamy eyes and an impressive physique. Never in his wildest dreams had he ever imagined the possibility of consuming those cravings.

In Clive's hands, Hans felt desired and loved. A handsome soldier found him attractive and wanted to take him. He wanted to be taken, to be held, to feel one with himself at last.

He didn't notice Clive sliding his chair closer to him. Nor did he notice Clive leaning back, unbuttoning his own trousers. His eyes were closed, and he was riding the waves of intense pleasure coursing through his body.

Suddenly, Hans felt his body shift to another plane – a state where all his senses coalesced into a forceful tempest overwhelming him. His breathing raced and his skin tightened. Suddenly, he felt his body explode, and he shuddered forcefully in Clive's hand. His heart pounded hard in his chest, and he sighed deeply.

Soon, his pulse returned to normal. He glanced over and noticed Clive was holding himself, moving his hand up and down. Moments before, Clive was a sexy and handsome man who made Hans' leg grow weak and melted his reserve. Now Clive's unambiguous determination to pleasure himself frightened Hans. It was an intentionality he couldn't embrace, one that represented deeply embedded disgrace. He shook his head, realizing the enormity of what he had done in front of a patient, a soldier, another man. He felt intense shame and compunction.

He murmured to Clive, "Don't."

Clive gave Hans a quizzical look, still stroking himself.

"It's not right," Hans said as he stood and walked around the side of the desk.

Clive kept rubbing himself, but he began to lose stiffness at Hans' disapproving words. He soon realized he wouldn't be able to come. He tucked his penis inside his trousers, buttoned up, and faced Hans.

"I'm sorry," Hans said.

"But what about you?" Clive asked, glancing at Hans' crotch.

"I didn't mean to. I lost control. I shouldn't have. You shouldn't either."

Clive had met other men who expressed guilt and remorse after sex, but usually not until both had come. He gave Hans a disappointed look.

"I'm sorry for what I did," Hans said, unable to look Clive in the eye.

"No need to be," Clive replied. "I like you."

Hans' face twitched. He liked Clive, too. He craved the sight of Clive's body each day during rounds. He loved Clive's humor, their discussions, and the way he felt young and alive in his presence. But now all he felt was regret for having let himself go, for having let the cravings take hold of him.

He retreated into his professional persona and said, "Well, I'll see you tomorrow when I make my rounds, right?"

Clive nodded. He stood there hoping Hans might say something else – express some gesture of friendship or affection. He didn't. Clive eventually turned and walked out of the door.

12

Chapter Twelve –
Questions

Mürren September 1917

Over the summer months, Clive's health improved. His breathing was clearer, and he regained physical strength. He continued to take in the sun on the terrace with other prisoners who were patients and enjoyed Dr. Weber's attentive care.

The slog of war, even if remote from the idyllic life in Mürren, proved weary for the prisoners who were unsure of the outcome of the hostilities. Would they ever return home? What would home be like? Would their wounds and disabilities limit future work, romance, and happiness?

Except for some of the officers, most of the enlisted men came from working-class or farming families. They passed time drinking beer, playing cards, and helping local farmers in exchange for pocket money and extra food. Clive was different. He had an active mind and was a voracious reader. When prisoners were allowed to

135

travel to nearby Interlaken or Thun, he raced to local bookstores, where he used his meager stipend to purchase new titles.

Back in Mürren, he proudly laid each new acquisition on his cot and hoped Hans would ask questions. Hans missed the stimulation of his professional circle in Bern and found the handsome prisoner a delightful distraction — physically and intellectually. Each new book became an opportunity for a visit to Hans' office where brandy lubricated discussion and the predictable exchange of affections.

Hans' guilt and shame were intractable, and Clive learned how to navigate their time together. The longer the discussion of a topic, the more excited Hans became, undoubtedly rehearsing in his mind how he might seduce Clive without it appearing too intentional. Clive watched Hans' longing mount and the conversation shift to more suggestive comments. A brush of the arm or a pat of the hand evolved into longer caresses. Legs pressed against each other, and elbows found convenient resting places as the two of them leaned over a manuscript and traced words with their fingers.

Looking up from the text, Hans was usually the first to lean into Clive and give him a kiss. Although Hans quickly lost control, Clive learned to orchestrate things so that he, Clive, came before Hans did. After climaxing, Hans would collapse into a sea of remorse and guilt and abruptly end their time together. The regret and disapproval in Hans' eyes haunted Clive.

Clive knew some of his comrades released sexual tension with one another, meeting up in a barn or behind a shed and jerking off together. It was transactional and physical, nothing more. Clive felt he and Hans had something different, something deeper. He loved Hans and hoped Hans loved him, too.

As a teen, Clive worried about his inclinations. He kept hoping they might be transitory, but his attraction to his male classmates continued. He never acted on his feelings and did everything he could to appear normal, going to dances with girls and talking about marriage and a future family with his buddies. The war was, oddly, a reprieve from the pressure his family put on him to find a suitable wife and take up a profession. He had a few casual exchanges with fellow soldiers during training, but nothing felt significant until he met Hans.

Hans' moral sentiments worried Clive. He wondered if Hans might be right, that men having sex with men was wrong, unnatural, immoral. When he went to the bookstores in Interlaken, he scoured the shelves for books on sexuality and psychology. There weren't many titles to choose from, but occasionally a book or magazine appeared with chapters or articles by Jung, Freud, and their students. Clive purchased everything he could get his hands on and carefully concealed them from his fellow soldiers.

From what he could surmise, Freud believed that children have a sexual drive that is bisexual, one that doesn't yet have a heterosexual or homosexual pattern. During adolescence, the child undergoes psychological development that includes the determination of sexual attraction. The normal development, according to Freud, is heterosexual. But some adolescents don't develop in the same way. They develop what he called an inverted sexuality, an attraction to people of the same sex.

Freud was intrigued by other scientists, one of them being Magnus Hirschfeld, from Berlin, who believed there were variations in human sexuality – with some people born homosexual and others born heterosexual. Freud and others wondered if there might be some underlying biological or organic basis for homosexuality. Freud never endorsed that theory, but Hirschfeld did.

Jung, Freud, Hirschfeld, and others were unanimous in their criticism of laws that criminalized homosexuality. In essence, they endorsed the view that homosexuality wasn't something immoral or dangerous for society.

Clive was encouraged by what he read and tried to engage Hans in discussions. Hans bristled each time Clive brought up the topic. He considered talking about it disgusting and inappropriate and continued to maintain that what they were doing was wrong and that he would try to be better. Of course, nothing changed.

Hans' remorse and guilt weighed heavily on Clive. He began to observe his fellow prisoners, wondering if others might be so inclined and be interested in more than a quick sexual exchange. On the terrace where TB patients took in the sun, Clive would excuse himself and go to the toilets. He walked along the line of chaises filled with young men. While many were not particularly handsome or in good shape, a few caught his attention. He took his time making his way to the facilities, hoping to catch a roving eye or glance. There was one – a certain young man named Harry. Harry was aptly named. He was a burly guy with an enviable physique and a warm smile. He and Clive shared glances. Clive observed his routine and activities and noticed he liked to hike and ski.

During a warm period in September, a local guide announced he would lead a hike to the upper slopes above Mürren. Clive's TB symptoms had subsided considerably, and he was restless. When he discovered Harry was joining the group, he signed up as well.

Early in the morning, ten comrades joined the guide, hiking first through the lower forests and then making their way above the tree line to the rocky slopes above. Harry walked alongside several men who had been part of his battalion. They laughed and told jokes as they trailed the gnarly guide leading them forward.

Clive brought up the rear, taking in the beautiful vistas and glancing periodically at glaciers above them. They continued to climb higher. The air became thinner, and Clive grew lightheaded. At one point, Harry glanced back at Clive and noticed his distress. He excused himself from his friends and approached Clive.

"Williams. Are you okay? You look pale."

"Yes. I just need to take deeper breaths. Dr. Weber is always reminding me I need to do that."

Harry nodded and waited as Clive expanded his chest and inhaled deeply.

"Why don't you sit for a moment," Harry suggested. He then glanced up at the others and said, "Let's take a break."

The guide halted their progress and encouraged everyone to stretch and drink some water. Harry remained with Clive, who slowly began to breathe normally.

"I think I'm okay," Clive noted, embarrassed that he had succumbed to his underlying condition. He stood. Harry placed his hand on Clive's shoulder, making sure he was stable. He nodded to the guide, and they all continued their trek up the mountain.

"Thanks," Clive said warmly to Harry. "You're very kind."

"We're all in this together. I have my days, too."

Clive couldn't imagine Harry becoming weak or pale or having to take a break. He glanced down at Harry's muscular legs pressing against the fabric of his hiking shorts. Harry's chest was broad and full, rising and falling with each breath he took. Clive gave him a second glance and murmured to himself, "Hmm. Interesting. He's handsome and thoughtful."

The group climbed a steep section, following an almost imperceptible trail that switched back and forth between boulders and scrubby vegetation. A few mountain goats grazed in the distance. They arrived at a small lake that had formed from the melting snow higher up. The guide suggested they take a break, have a snack, and then they would continue higher, to a peak called the Schilthorn.

Clive unwrapped some cheese and sausage from a small backpack he had been carrying. He reached down, cupped his hands, and took several sips from the clear mountain lake.

"It's so beautiful, no?" Harry remarked as he sat near Clive.

"I know. Just like home!" Clive replied, chuckling.

Harry's eyes turned red. He had become terribly homesick as the months progressed.

Clive noticed and said, "Did I say something wrong?"

Harry nodded no, choked with emotion. Finally, he managed to say, "I'm just so grateful we're alive. But as beautiful as this is, I can't wait to go home."

"Do you have someone waiting for you?" Clive inquired.

"I did, but I found out she moved on with someone else."

"Sorry to hear. That's unfair."

Harry nodded and took a bite of cheese, wiping a tear from his cheek. "And you?"

"No one," Clive replied in a murmur.

"Haven't met the right woman yet?"

Clive nodded without comment. While he thought Harry might have had similar inclinations given a few glances they had exchanged over the past few months, his remark about a rogue girlfriend back home threw him off track. Clive observed Harry carefully, looking for clues they might share similar sentiments. Harry's tousled hair, scruffy beard, and country accent suggested a straight shooter, a no-nonsense manly soldier eager to return home, marry, and start a family. But there was a certain flair in the way he assembled his bread and cheese and the manner in which he peeled his pear that caught Clive's attention.

Harry's body was burly, but his hands were elegant and graceful. His nose was long and sexy, and he had a cute mouth – round and boyish. Clive was mesmerized as Harry consumed his lunch and wondered if there wasn't something under the surface, another identity clamoring to find expression.

"What will you do when you get home? I mean, in terms of work?" Clive inquired of Harry.

Harry glanced off into the distance, deep in thought. "My father is a coal miner. I guess that's my future. My girlfriend, Diane, found someone with better prospects, a veterinarian."

"You must have other options, too."

"I don't know. What will happen after the war? Everyone needs coal, and there's plenty of work in the mines."

"But you could train in some other trade or go to college."

"That's not for me," Harry remarked, cutting a slice of the juicy pear and placing it in his mouth.

Clive couldn't imagine someone as handsome as Harry not having lofty dreams, not imagining a life more sophisticated than that of his parents. He pressed him further, "Have you ever thought about other jobs or professions? If you could be anything, what would it be?"

A warm smile spread across Harry's face, and his eyes sparkled. "I would love to be a teacher. I never knew this kind of world existed. Look at us! We're in a pristine Alpine village where there's a whole different culture – different language, food, customs, looks. I'd like to share that with kids."

Clive detected the excitement in Harry's voice and said, "Tell me more. What draws you to that?"

"I want kids to dream big, to know there's another world out there."

"Why doesn't that apply to you?"

Harry looked perplexed, almost as if he had seen a phantom. He shook his head no. "It's too late for me."

"Why do you say that?"

"The war, our injuries, the things we've seen. I don't know how to describe it. It's taken the magic out of life. The horror seems so overwhelming. I can't seem to see beyond it – at least not for me."

Harry's pain and internal discomfort were palpable, and Clive wished he could reach over and embrace him. He knew how soothing a man's touch could be. Men were combative, forceful, aggressive, and inimical. When a man touched another man tenderly, affectionately, warmly, it was is if all the hostility of the world vanished. Hans had been that for Clive. Clive wondered if he could be that for Harry.

Clive pondered whether to make a small gesture of affection when, suddenly, the guide said to the group, "Men, we need to move on. If we are going to make it to the Schilthorn and back by nightfall, we need to continue forward. Let's pack our things and prepare for the rest of our ascent."

Everyone stood, stretched, and adjusted their clothes, poles, and backpacks. They continued their march up the mountain. Clive continued to feel weak and wondered if he should turn back. Harry had returned to his friends up front, although he glanced back from time to time to check on Clive. At one point, Harry looked back, and Clive shook his head. He couldn't continue.

Harry walked back and said, "You don't look good. Why don't we wait here for them to go up and return?"

"I don't want to hold you back. I'm okay. I'll rest down there by the lake."

"I'll go with you."

"Stay with your friends."

"No. In fact, I'm feeling weak myself. I'll stay with you."

Clive gave him an incredulous look and nodded. Harry walked up to the guide and explained that he and Clive couldn't proceed. They would remain at the lake or begin to make their way back to town. The guide had a worried look on his face, but realized there was no way the two could continue. He nodded.

The group moved on, and Clive and Harry made their way back to the small lake. They sat on some large boulders and watched as the small group proceeded up the slopes. They became smaller and smaller and eventually blended in with the landscape of rocks and ice above them.

"You don't need to stay here with me. I'll be fine," Clive said to Harry.

"I wasn't feeling well myself. I don't mind sitting here and taking in the views."

Clive raised his brow, wondering why Harry would give up a trek with his buddies for a more protracted conversation with him. "So, you're not feeling that well, either?"

Harry shook his head no. "My mind says I'm twenty and invincible, but my chest labors to take in air, and I find myself weak at times."

Clive chuckled. Harry had described his sentiments exactly. "Will we ever be free of this?"

"I hope so," Harry replied. He paused and then added, "What do you think of Dr. Weber? Does he know what he's doing? Are we getting the right care?"

Clive felt his heart flutter thinking about Hans – not so much about his medical care, but about the conversations they had and the intimacy they shared. He felt himself blush and looked off evasively into the distance. He said, "He seems competent, and I feel better than when we first arrived."

"Me, too. Did you have any wounds?"

"Shrapnel in the leg," Clive replied. He stuck out his leg and pointed to a few scars. "And you?"

"A laceration of my hip," Harry said, unbuckling his shorts and pulling them down slightly to show Clive a large scar on his side and buttocks.

Clive felt his heart race. Harry's scar was frightening, but his muscular, hairy buttocks were impressive and terribly sexy. Clive wondered if Harry knew how provocative his little gesture had been. Was he toying with Clive?

Harry leaned back on his arms. He unbuttoned his shirt and took it off, exposing his hairy and muscular chest to the warm sunshine. "Do you think this works?"

Clive knew he meant to ask whether heliotherapy was effective in eradicating TB, but all Clive could think of was how effective Harry's state of undress was in causing him to stir.

"Hmm," Clive replied, preoccupied with the mounting feelings he had for the handsome man reclining in front of him. "I hope so." He leaned back, faced the sun, and felt its warmth.

"Back to Dr. Weber. Do you think he's okay?" Harry pressed Clive.

"In what sense? He seems to know a lot about our condition and how to treat it."

"Yes, he does. He also seems very inquisitive," Harry remarked, raising his brow.

"I imagine that's how he figures out if we're getting better or not."

"Hmm," Harry began. "Sometimes I feel like he's too nosy. He asks a lot of questions and feels around a lot."

Clive blushed. He gazed at Harry and realized that he was one of the handsome men. If Hans had made advances on him, Clive, he must have undoubtedly found Harry equally attractive. Maybe he had made Harry uncomfortable with where he touched and how he touched, maybe even in the way he looked at Harry, peered into his eyes or asked personal questions. Clive didn't know how to respond to Harry. He paused.

Before Clive could respond, Harry interjected, "Dr. Weber seems to like you."

"What?" Clive replied with a fake surprised tone and expression.

"He spends more time with you. You both seem to have a lot to talk about."

"He does that with everyone," Clive noted evasively.

"No. I'm pretty sure you get special treatment."

Clive now began to perspire, worried that Harry had seen something or had been taking notice over the past months. Maybe Harry's glances in his direction were not evidence of an interest or affinity but a curiosity about what might be developing between him and Dr. Weber.

"He asks about the books I'm reading."

"Hmm," Harry murmured, not entirely convinced that explained things. He noticed Clive's discomfort and added, "It's nice when people share interests. I'm afraid I'm not very interesting in that sense."

Clive wasn't sure what Harry meant. He interjected, "You make friends quickly. You like to hike, ski, and play rugby."

"But I don't have anyone with whom I can have deeper conversations. You know, like we're having." Harry smiled warmly at Clive. The sun made his face radiant, and his deep brown eyes were alluring.

Clive wondered if Harry was trying to solicit Clive's affection in some way. Clive was about to say something when Harry added, "Some guys take it the wrong way, if you know what I mean."

Clive checked himself and murmured, "Hmm. You mean if you have a deeper conversation?"

Harry nodded. "If you start talking about philosophy or emotions or things like that, they think you're soft."

Clive was certifiably bewildered. Handsome Harry had taken off his shirt and was reclining in the sun. He had initiated a thoughtful conversation, but he wanted to make sure Clive knew there was nothing more to it. Clive wasn't sure who Harry was trying to convince of his innocence – himself or Clive.

Clive froze, not sure what to say next. He pulled his knees up against his chest and squeezed them with his arms. He gazed out at the horizon, at the peaks across the valley.

Then Harry interjected. "Not that I have a problem with that sort of thing."

"What do you mean?" Clive asked.

"You know, if a bloke likes another bloke."

"Ahh. Yes. A complicated matter."

"It's just not my thing."

Clive nodded. "It can be confusing."

"So, what do you like to read?" Harry asked.

"A variety of things – novels, history, philosophy, psychology."

"And Dr. Weber likes those things, too?"

Clive nodded.

"It must be wonderful to find common interests with someone from another country – someone who speaks another language and who thinks in other ways. It's like another you, but in a different world, a reflection of yourself in a different hue or light or atmosphere."

"I didn't realize you were so poetic," Clive remarked to Harry, certifiably intrigued by his insights.

"I just describe what I observe." Clive blushed. Harry noticed and added, "Don't worry. It doesn't bother me. In fact, I'm intrigued. I wish I had what you two have."

Clive shook his head to convey surprise, even though Harry had hit the nail on the head.

"We don't agree on a lot of things," Clive said, hoping to make his and Hans' relationship seem more intellectual and focused on academic topics.

Harry saw right through Clive's attempt to minimize his and Hans' relationship. He raised his brow and said, "I imagine you challenge him. I can tell you are clever. You're a smart bloke. But you're sensitive, too. That must scare him."

Clive shook his head, incredulous as to how accurate Harry was in describing his and Hans' relationship. Harry must have read Clive's bewilderment and added, "Yeah. I know. On the surface, people wouldn't think I'm all that perceptive."

Clive chuckled. "You don't know how accurate your observations are."

"I can see it in your eyes. Sadness and frustration. It's what I felt when Diane told me she was moving on."

"I'm sorry for you," Clive said warmly.

"It's okay. I'll find someone else when I go back."

"I'm sure you will. You're very handsome and thoughtful."

"So, what will you do?" Harry asked Clive, giving him a curious look.

"I don't know. I feel as if I don't belong. What I'm attracted to, I can't have. What I can have, I don't want. Home doesn't feel like home, but I'm not at home here, either."

"I've thought a lot about our situation here," Harry began. "The war seems so far off. We're in a place that is serene, beautiful, and comfortable. Yet the world around us is unraveling. It's like we are in a parallel universe. We can't even see the other universe, although we read about it. We've been there, and we carry its horrific memories with us. But we can't touch it now even if we tried. Your situation must be even worse. Not only do you share this separate world with the rest of the prisoners, but you have your own parallel world within ours. You must enter it from time to time, but it isn't home. But neither is this. I can't imagine what it's like to never feel like you belong."

Clive's eyes turned red. No one had ever described so accurately the dilemma he faced, the anguish his love and affection caused him on a daily basis.

"What should I do?" Clive asked, struggling to speak between sobs. He had never asked someone for advice about life, but he felt like Harry understood his situation like no one else.

"Right now, nothing different. Enjoy the opportunity you have. Dr. Weber likes to talk with you. I imagine he enjoys other things as well."

Clive nodded slightly, wiping the tears away from his eyes.

Harry continued, "When the war is over, it won't be for you. We will all go home, but there isn't one for you. Maybe our confinement is training for you, a place to figure out how to live in two worlds at the same time."

"I don't want that," Clive said.

"Who would? In the same way that we are here as prisoners until the world around us changes, there's nothing you can do but live in two worlds until the world changes. And I don't see that happening soon."

"How did you become so wise, so insightful?" Clive asked Harry.

Harry glanced off into the distance, deep in thought. He turned back to Clive and said, "I've always been very observant. I watched my father and mother work hard. Both of them dreamed of a better world for themselves and for their children, but they could never break free. The weight of life kept them anchored in our coal-mining town. One of my uncles was different. He was a miner, too. But he read books, traveled to other worlds in his mind, and never married. He had a friend. They seemed close chums. Mom and Dad whispered about Uncle Ben and his friend Bobby. I was curious and intrigued. It was as if Uncle Ben had carved out a special world within our world, one that had a unique beauty, light, and sparkle to it. I wanted to visit Uncle Ben's world, but only as a tourist. It wasn't my world, but it represented the possibility of other worlds. I wish I had his courage. I wish I had yours."

Clive looked off across the valley at the mountainous landscape. From their high vantage point, the horizon was like a world of possibilities, a land of lofty peaks piercing the blue sky. Clive took a deep breath and felt inspired to dream big. He hoped one day the world would rise up to meet his imagination. He sensed it was inevitable. He just wasn't sure how long it would take.

13

Chapter Thirteen – The Inevitable

Mürren Winter 2007

Later, at dinner, Max approached Elliott's table after coffee and dessert had been served. He held his hands behind his back and bowed formally.

"Mr. Williams, could I offer you an after-dinner brandy in the parlor?" Max's voice was silky and warm. He continued. "You know, as a way to compensate for the lack of nightclubs in our village."

"Mr. Weber, that is very kind of you. Of course," Elliott said, winking at Max.

Max glanced back at the kitchen. Sofia was busy stacking dishes. Most of the families had retired to their rooms, and the hotel staff were cleaning tables and helping Sofia prepare the room for breakfast the next day.

Max and Elliott wandered into the parlor. Max took some logs and threw them on the fire. Sparks rose into the chimney and orange flames singed the edge of the fresh wood. Max opened the credenza, pulled out two glasses, and filled them with brandy. He handed one to Elliott and said, "Cheers."

They sat in front of the fire. "So, what did you think?" Max began.

"It was a great day. Thanks for accompanying me. It was very kind of you."

"It was my pleasure. I don't get out often enough. I'm glad to have had the opportunity."

"Is Sofia joining us?"

Max nodded no. "She's busy."

"You don't have to help?"

"It's my free pass."

Elliott raised his brow. He wasn't sure what a free pass included and decided not to ask for more information. He said, "Don't let me keep you up past your bedtime!"

Max twitched. Suddenly, he looked restless. He leaned forward and gazed into the fire. Elliott was sitting to his right in a comfortable stuffed chair. Max lifted his hand and put it on Elliott's knee. "You were quite the skier today! You surprised me."

Elliott could feel the warmth in Max's hand. It was almost hot. He felt his heart begin to melt as the heat traversed his body and filled his chest. It had been too long since someone had touched him affectionately.

Max patted Elliott's knee in an attempt to make the gesture seem playful - two buddies sharing a moment after a day on the slopes. But, in fact, for Max, it was a frightening attempt to show affection to a man.

Elliott looked into Max's eyes. They shimmered in the ambient light of the room. They were full of longing. Elliott knew what Max wanted, but he feared it came at a price. Sofia was only steps away, and Max had a mercurial temperament. Elliott had been there before. Hot guy comes on strong and regrets it later. He was alone in a small town in a small inn. It was too risky.

"I'm sorry for being such a sissy up at the top," Elliott said, hoping to distract Max from his underlying intentions.

"I get it. We are all afraid of something."

Elliott joined Max in gazing into the fire. He swirled the brandy, breathed in its rich aromas, and then took a sip. Still facing the fireplace, he asked, "What are you afraid of, Max?"

They both slowly turned toward each other. There was terror in Max's eyes. Elliott knew what he craved and what he feared. Max didn't answer the question. Instead, he asked, "Sofia said you have some postcards and letters from your grandfather in your room. Could I see them?"

Elliott raised his brows. He knew it wasn't postcards Max wanted to see.

"Sure," he said, playing along with the pretext. A voice in his head said, "Don't do it." But his heart was pounding, and he could feel desire rising within.

They stood and climbed the stairs to Elliott's room. He opened the door and let Max in. Max glanced around the familiar space, one he had cleaned, repaired, painted, and appointed over the years. Elliott went to the small table on the other side of the room and picked up several postcards, images from the very mountains they had skied earlier in the day. He turned around to hand them to Max, but he found that Max had walked up close behind him and was only inches away. His eyes were intense and hungry. He leaned toward Elliott and gave him a warm, moist kiss.

Elliott let the cards fall on the floor. He peered into Max's eyes and felt his body stir. He hesitated a moment and then kissed him back. Max reached behind Elliott and squeezed his buttocks. Elliott moaned.

Elliott glanced around the room – nervous and apprehensive. Max reached up and caressed the side of Elliott's jaw, turning it so that Elliott faced him. Elliott could feel Max's breath on his face, the sweet aroma of brandy floating in the air between them. Elliott felt his skin tighten as Max kissed the side of his neck and ran his hot lips down toward his clavicle.

Elliott expressed hesitation, murmuring, "*Wir sollten nicht.*"

Max held his finger up to Elliott's mouth and pressed it against his lips. "Shh," he whispered.

Elliott rested his hand on Max's chest, feeling the tightening muscles pressing against the smooth fabric. Elliott began slowly to unbutton Max's shirt. His chest was smooth and warm. Elliott slid his hand inside the folds of the fabric, feeling the contours of Max's pecs. He glanced down and saw that Max had become aroused.

After unbuttoning the last button, Elliott continued farther down and unzipped Max's trousers. As he did, he could feel Max's hardness against his hand. He wanted to reach in and take hold of Max, but he feared that would be pushing him too far, too quickly. He simply stared into Max's eyes.

Max took hold of Elliott's hand and guided it inside the front of his trousers, against his hardness. Elliott had been given permission, and he reached inside Max's undershorts and took hold of him. Elliott's pulse raced.

Without saying anything, Max pushed Elliott gently toward the bed. Neither wanted to pierce the silence laden with mounting desire. At the edge of the mattress, he gave Elliott another nudge, and Elliott fell back onto the bed. Max reached down and unbuckled Elliott's belt, unzipped his pants, and rubbed his hands over Elliott's erection. He kneeled on the bed, straddling Elliott, and leaned over him.

Elliott tugged at Max's underwear so that his impressive assets sprung free of the fabric and dangled over him. Elliott stroked him, and Max arched his back. He lowered himself to the side of Elliott, reaching inside Elliott's underwear to feel the hardness underneath.

In his wildest imagination, Elliott hadn't dreamed his day on the slopes would end this way. Max had seemed reticent and reserved even if friendly at times. He was inscrutable. Elliott wondered if that wasn't a symptom of a deep, dark current that coursed through his ski buddy. He leaned over and breathed in the faint but intoxicating scent rising from Max's moist skin.

Elliott looked into Max's eyes to take a read. He seemed exceptionally skilled at what he was doing, but Elliott hadn't picked up on any inclinations during the day. Was Max having a moment, discovering something new, or was Elliott one of many guests Max had managed to charm and seduce.

Despite Max's adroitness, and the craving in his eyes, Elliott could feel uncertainty in his hands – or at least he hoped there was uncertainty. He wanted to be special, to be a unique encounter, a breakthrough. If so, he feared the inevitable remorse that might follow. It was a small inn. He was at the beginning of his two-week vacation. He wasn't sure he could deal with regret and coldness from the handsome innkeeper.

"*Bist du dir sicher?*" Elliott asked, wanting to make sure Max was certain he wanted to move forward.

Max nodded yes.

Elliott extended his leg over Max's side, pressing his hardness up against Max's. The heat of their soft, sensitive skin next to each other sent charges through their bodies. Elliott nudged himself in between Max's legs. Max was hot and wet with perspiration. Elliott slid inside the space between Max's thighs. Max squeezed himself around Elliott's sex, throbbing in anticipation.

"You're so sexy," Elliott whispered into Max's ear. He observed the way Max's playful, thick hair rested on the back of his neck. He nuzzled his nose in it and began to work his way along Max's shoulder, caressing it with his warm lips.

Max stirred. He turned and took hold of Elliott's shoulders and pressed him down under him. He straddled him, his firm cock resting on Elliott's abdomen. He leaned over and, with his tongue, began to wet the edges of Elliott's pecs covered in soft, dark hair. He bit them playfully and felt Elliott's cock bob under him. "You're magnificent," Max said softly, warmly.

Elliott realized no straight man would say that and abandoned himself to the mounting desire he felt for Max and the determination he perceived in Max's eyes.

Max reclined on top of Elliott, encircled Elliott's luscious mouth with his own, and felt the wetness between them. He was in novel territory. He had taken charge; he was initiating things. He was conveying his affection without hesitation, without remorse.

Elliott glanced up at Max. His eyes were alive and there was delight in his smile. The distant and aloof innkeeper had a tenderness in his regard, an affection that made Elliott's heart melt. "I just want to eat you up," Max murmured, nuzzling his nose in the side of Elliott's neck. Their torsos slid as wet perspiration formed between them.

Max nudged himself deeper in between Elliott's legs. He clearly wanted to enter. Elliott spread his legs and relaxed. Max pressed harder and slowly, but firmly, slid in, filling Elliott's body with warmth and force. Elliott gazed at the man hovering over him, noticing the intense satisfaction filling his regard.

Max leaned up and took hold of Elliott, pressing and rubbing in just the right places to make Elliott tremble in pleasure. Max was in control, stroking Elliott with skill and thrusting himself inside. Elliott felt waves of intense pleasure begin to rise within. He placed his hands on the back of Max's buttocks and pulled him closer. He could feel Max throb inside of him. They both closed their eyes and relinquished all remaining hesitation, their bodies finding a shared rhythm.

Suddenly, they both came with a forceful climax, Max writhing inside Elliott and Elliott's hardness exploding between them.

Max collapsed, panting on top of Elliott, who relished the weight of this mysterious man on top of him. Elliott could feel Max's heart pounding and ran his hand over Max's back. A few moments later, Max slid off Elliott and lifted himself off the bed. He walked into the bathroom and washed up, wrapping a towel around his waist. He returned to the room and sat on the sofa. He reached into his trousers and pulled out a cigarette and lighter. He glanced toward Elliott and asked if he minded. "*Macht es dir etwas aus?*"

Elliott nodded no; it didn't bother him. He was elated that Max spoke to him in German. It was another sign of melting boundaries. He then asked if there was more brandy. "*Hat es noch mehr Brandy?*"

Max nodded, offering to retrieve it. "*Soll ich's holen?*"

"No. It would be better if I go downstairs and get it." Elliott put on his pants and shirt and tiptoed down the stairs, retrieving their glasses and the bottle of brandy.

When he returned, Max was thumbing through the postcards and photos Elliott had dropped on the floor. "This is amazing," he said, reading the note from Margrit to Clive and scanning a few other cards Hans had sent earlier, imploring Clive to come visit.

"Hmm," Elliott murmured. He poured them both a glass of brandy. "I always thought my grandfather had troubling feelings and thoughts about Mürren because of the war or because of a long-lost love, Margrit. But I've come to realize there were some cards from Hans, inviting Clive to visit."

"Yes, it would seem there must have been a strong connection between Hans and Clive," Max added, not sure how much to share with Elliott about what Sofia hypothesized when she read the medical chart.

Elliott took a sip of brandy, and Max took a drag of his cigarette. Elliott said, "It's so surreal. Our coming together."

"Hmm," Max murmured, nodding. He wondered what Clive looked like; if he would have found him handsome and what Hans saw in him. "It is all rather curious."

"How so?" Elliott inquired, furrowing his brows.

"I don't know. I didn't expect it."

"The uptight Englishman, right?"

Max blushed. That was exactly what he was thinking. However, Elliott had turned out more playful and vulnerable, and it turned Max on. He nodded and said softly, "It's a façade. You were quite spontaneous and playful on the slopes."

"It's such a different environment from work. There's something about being in the middle of nature – the mountains, the forests, the snow – that is transformative. And then, with skiing, you have to be in the moment. It's quite liberating."

"Hmm," Max murmured. "But I didn't expect that of you."

Elliott grinned, realizing Max had been observing him since his arrival. He said, "I found you handsome from the moment you greeted me. But you seemed inaccessible. Even today, on the cable car, you were inscrutable."

Max nodded pensively. Both sat quietly with their thoughts, each realizing they had penetrated the hard shell the other had erected. Neither knew what might come next and worried their respective armor might go back up sooner than later.

Max glanced around the room. Elliott noticed and remarked, "It must be strange to be in a guest room like this." At least, Elliott hoped it was strange for Max.

It was a new experience for Max, and Elliott's giving voice to the peculiarity of it all made his stomach flutter anxiously. His face jerked, and he looked evasively away from Elliott. A wave of guilt washed over him. He found Elliott surprisingly interesting and easy to be with. Sitting with him and having a glass of brandy felt like the most natural thing he could imagine and, at the same time, unusual and unexpected. He was in a guest room, with a guest, and the realization of that unnerved him.

"So, are you okay?" Elliott asked as he observed Max grow unsettled.

Max nodded unconvincingly. He glanced down elusively at the handful of photos and postcards he had used as a pretext to see if he might seduce Elliott. He thumbed through them.

"So, is this your grandfather?" Max asked, pointing to an individual in one of the photos.

Elliott leaned over to look at the image. "Yes. That's him."

"I can see how he would have turned Hans' and Margrit's heads. He's striking – just like his grandson!"

Elliott blushed. He then said, "And that must be your great grandfather, since he's wearing a doctor's coat."

Max nodded. He continued to gaze at the photo, rubbing his fingers over the figures. He wondered what it must have been like during the war and how the men endured the long confinement.

Elliott continued his query and asked, "Do you know who these other people are?"

Max nodded no. He held the photo up closer to observe the individuals. There was one man not in a uniform nor a doctor's coat. Max peered at the images and said, "I think that might be my great grandfather's brother, Georg."

Elliott leaned over Max's shoulder to take a look. Elliott perceived a sudden change in Max's demeanor, more restless and agitated. He continued to peer at the photo and his hands started to tremble. His eyes turned red and sullen. There was a look of dread spreading across his face.

Abruptly, he stood up and went into the bathroom to put out his cigarette. He took a long sip of the brandy and began to pace. He dropped the towel and slipped on his undershorts, pants, and shirt.

He circled the room a couple of times, quietly and pensively. Suddenly, he said, "I have to go."

"What's wrong?" Elliott asked with alarm.

"Nothing," Max said without elaboration. He couldn't give voice to his feelings. They were terrifying.

"Max, something is the matter. What's up?"

"I can't talk about it," he said as he pressed his fingers into his temples, clearly anxious and in pain.

"Sure, you can. Tell me what's troubling you."

"I can't." Max walked hastily out of the room.

14

⚜

Chapter Fourteen – Family Man

Mürren November 1917

Late afternoon golden light beamed through the dining-room window. Margrit made last-minute adjustments to the plates, napkins, and silverware on the old wooden table. She squeezed the stems of a bunch of dried cone flowers and let them fall naturally into the vase. Candles were ready to be lit once the guest arrived.

Hans fussed nervously in the parlor. He readied glasses and a bottle of whiskey on the credenza and poked several logs burning in the fireplace.

Clive approached the modest chalet at the edge of town. He glanced up at the mountain peaks towering overhead in the dusky light. They had received a fresh blanket of snow.

He knocked on the door of the apartment. Soon, Hans opened it and stood beaming in the doorway. He wore a thick wool sweater, a light blue shirt, and dark slacks. Clive caught his breath. He had never seen Hans in anything but a physician's coat. He was

160

more handsome than usual. His cheeks were flushed, his hair tousled, and his intoxicating cologne swirled about in the mix of indoor and outdoor air as they both stood facing each other in the doorway.

"Come in," Hans said fondly, squeezing Clive's hands warmly.

Margrit approached from behind Hans. She wore a red and white apron over a simple light blue dress. Her skin seemed luminous in the glow of the fireplace just inside the door.

Hans stepped back as Clive entered. "Clive, this is my wife, Margrit. Margrit, Clive."

"Enchanted," Clive said, shaking her hand warmly. He handed her a small bouquet of flowers.

"*Danke schön*," she expressed as she took the flowers and gestured for him to enter.

"Let me take your coat," Hans said, as he placed his hands affectionately on Clive's shoulder.

Hans helped Clive remove his coat and hung it on the decorative hall tree just inside the door.

Clive glanced around the room and said, "It's so warm and cozy."

"Come have sit," Margrit said in broken English. "*Etwas zu trinken?*"

Clive nodded and walked toward a large stuffed chair next to the fire. Hans reached for a bottle and nodded to Clive. "Some whiskey?"

Clive nodded. "That would be nice."

Margrit excused herself and went into the kitchen. Hans poured them both a glass of whiskey and sat in a chair across from Clive.

Hans felt himself tremble. He found Clive irresistible. His dark, wavy hair glistened in the light of the oil lamps. His dark brown eyes were exceptionally alluring. He wasn't sure what to say. He awkwardly began, "So, is everything fine with your comrades?"

Clive didn't want to talk about his comrades. He wanted to find out more about Hans. Who was he in his other life - in his life as a civilian, as a husband, as a father?

"They're good. And you?"

Hans looked nervously around the room. Suddenly, a three-year-old appeared. "Ahh. Conrad!" Hans said playfully. The boy jumped on his lap and played with the buttons on his sweater.

Margrit had followed him and stood in the doorway. Hans said, "Clive, this is my son, Conrad. *Conrad, dies ist Herr Williams.*"

Conrad glanced shyly away from Clive and leaped off Hans' lap and ran to Margrit, grabbing hold of her apron.

"*Er ist so süss,*" Clive remarked.

"He is indeed sweet, and he is a handful!" Hans replied, chuckling.

"*Margrit. Komm und trink etwas mit uns.*"

Margrit lifted Conrad onto her hips and walked toward the sofa. She sat while Hans stood and poured her a drink. He handed it to her, and she lifted it and said, "*Zum Wohl.*"

Clive realized Margrit's English was limited, and his German equally so.

Hans had already prepared himself to serve as a translator, but as Margrit and Clive both sat in the same room, he realized there was more than language he would have to bridge.

Margrit scrutinized Clive. He was a prisoner of war – not exactly an enemy but someone representing something foreign and covert. He seemed oddly normal, pleasant, handsome, educated. Hans told her stories about his patients — their injuries, disfigurement, and intractable cases of TB. Clive was robust and had a warm smile and handsome face. He didn't seem ill. He didn't seem to fit the mold.

"*Sind Sie Engländer?*" she asked.

Clive nodded.

"*Und was sind Sie von Beruf?*" Margrit asked about his profession.

"*Soldat.*"

"But when you go back, what will you do?" Hans interjected, hoping to elicit more information from Clive.

"I am not sure. I haven't given it much thought." In fact, in combat, he was convinced he would die. It was only recently, convalescing in the Alps, that Clive gave himself permission to imagine a future.

"I could see you as a teacher," Hans noted. "You're well read and know a lot about history, art, and politics."

Clive blushed.

Margrit glanced at her husband, whose eyes were fixed on Clive. She sensed his interest and fascination with their guest.

"*Entschuldigung. Ich muss in die Küche.*" Margrit excused herself to attend to things in the kitchen. She stood and carried Conrad with her.

Hans took a deep breath and peered into Clive's dark brown eyes. They were serious, pensive, inscrutable. Clive felt the intensity of Hans' regard and began to perspire.

"Margrit seems very nice," Clive remarked nervously.

"Yes. She's wonderful."

"How did you meet?"

"Through extended family, back in Bern."

Clive nodded.

"Her father is a doctor, too."

"Ahh. It runs in the family, then?"

"Hm hmm," Hans murmured, taking a sip of whiskey.

"She must be very proud of you."

Hans blushed. Clive wondered if Hans feared she saw through him.

"And Conrad, he looks just like you!" Clive added.

Hans relaxed and grinned. He said, "He's more like his mother. Curious, clever, perceptive."

Clive felt his heart pound. He hoped she wasn't too perceptive.

Margrit appeared in the doorway. "*Es ist bereit.*"

"Shall we go to the dining room?" Hans said as he stood, finished his glass of whiskey, and gestured for Clive to follow him.

Margrit pointed to a chair for Clive. Conrad sat in a highchair off to the side. He was already consuming his dinner, his legs rocking underneath him. Hans and Clive sat, and Margrit brought in a bowl filled with a savory soup. She returned to the kitchen and brought back a platter with bread and cheese.

Clive glanced around the room and said, "The table is beautiful, Margrit. The candles and flowers - it's so warm and such a contrast to things at the hotel. Thanks for inviting me." He glanced at Hans to translate. He did, and Margrit blushed.

Hans poured some wine into glasses on the table and proposed a toast. "To new friends that this tragic war has brought together."

"To new friends," Clive said with his glass raised.

"*Auf die Freundschaft!*" Margrit added, glancing back and forth between Hans and Clive.

Margrit passed the food around. Everyone took a healthy portion. Clive took his first spoonful and said, "*E Guete!*"

Margrit nodded, surprised Clive seemed to have picked up a few Swiss German words. "You patient?" Margrit asked in her limited English.

"Yes. I'm Hans' patient."

"Good doctor? Hans?"

"Very good. He is smart, thoughtful, and caring."

Margrit looked at her husband, who self-consciously translated Clive's remarks. She smiled at Clive.

Hans' decision to move to Mürren to take care of the prisoners had surprised her. She always wondered if he had become a doctor out of pressure from his parents – that perhaps he really didn't like the work. It was encouraging to hear a patient speak well of him.

Margrit was curious and wanted to ask, 'Why you? Why are you here?' Hans had never brought a patient to their home in Mürren or, for that matter, in Bern. When he proposed inviting Clive, she welcomed the idea at first. The local townsfolk were friendly, but reserved. They had few social opportunities, so the idea of having a dinner guest excited her.

She watched her husband. Male companionship confounded her. Men were more cerebral than women, and she always wondered what drew them together – whether it was sports, work, or politics. With women, there was a plethora of topics to discuss and emotions to share. Hans was ordinarily impenetrable. Their exchanges were largely practical – how to raise their son, what to buy at the market, how to organize the household. Hans showed little interest in discussing feelings. He told her he loved her. He was devoted and stable and a good household companion.

She wondered what common interests a doctor and a soldier might have. She studied the two of them, hoping to detect something – a look, an expression, a reference. Nothing.

"Rugby? You play?" she asked, wondering if sports might be their connection, although Hans wasn't particularly athletic.

Clive nodded, glancing at Hans.

"Ski?" she pressed more.

Clive nodded, more excitedly. "I like the winter."

In German, Hans told Margrit, "Clive is very athletic. He is popular amongst his comrades – playing rugby, skiing, hiking."

She sighed, relieved that perhaps Clive was friendly with everyone. "*Gefällt es Ihnen hier?*"

Clive nodded. "Yes. I like it here. Good care from the Swiss and from Doctor Hans!"

"The other *Soldaten*. How are they?" Margrit realized she had a window into Hans' other world through Clive, and her curiosity was intense.

"Hmm," Clive began tentatively, not sure what Margrit's question was. He glanced at Hans to translate. "There are many. They are sick. They are bored. They are young."

Hans translated. Margrit continued her line of questioning. "*Und die Tanzabende?*"

"Ah, yes. The dances are a wonderful distraction for us. The people in Interlaken and other towns have been very nice to organize those."

"Girls?"

"Yes. Swiss girls." Clive replied with a warm smile.

"You?"

Clive wanted to ask Margrit if she was asking if he was a Swiss girl, but he knew the question would mortify Hans, even if it was delivered as a joke. Now he knew Margrit's motive, the question behind the questions.

"*Noch niemand.* No one yet."

"*Warum?*" Margrit asked tenaciously. "*Jemand zu Hause?*"

Clive glanced at his hand and lifted it. He had no ring. "*Ich bin schüchtern.*"

Evasively, Margrit picked up a piece of cheese and took a sip of wine. She was certain Clive was not shy, even if he had said so. He was charming, warm, and a conversationalist.

Margrit glanced at Hans and said, "*Meine Cousine Rita in Bern.*"

"*Nein,*" he replied gruffly to Margrit's suggestion of introducing Clive to Rita, her cousin.

Clive picked up a piece of cheese and a slice of bread. He could play the same game. "If your cousin Rita is as beautiful as you, I would love to meet her."

Hans looked askance at Clive and turned to Margrit, who waited for the translation. Hans found it difficult to translate the compliment Clive had made. He mumbled something to her, and she blushed.

They shifted to other topics – the war, the upcoming winter, Conrad's milestones, and the paucity of food and fuel. Conrad grew restless, and Margrit stared at Hans, who nodded no. He was not going to get their son ready for bed.

In a huff, Margrit stood and reached for Conrad. "*Zeit für ins Bett.*" She continued to stare at Hans.

In German, Hans said, "Clive and I will clear the table and do the dishes."

Margrit returned an astonished look at Hans' offer. She took Conrad upstairs to his room. Hans and Clive took the bowls into the kitchen. They stood next to each other in front of the sink, their hips pressed against one another. Hans felt his legs go weak. He turned and looked imploringly into Clive's eyes.

Clive returned the gaze.

"It's nice to see you in your element. Such a family man!" Clive said, winking at Hans.

Hans turned red and creased his brows. He was terrified that Clive might betray something to Margrit.

"Hand me the dishes. I'll wash. You dry."

"Yes. *Herr Kommandant!*"

Hans smiled. He removed his sweater and rolled his sleeves, reaching his hands in the soapy water to wipe the bowls and plates. He handed the first to Clive, who took it, grazing Hans' hand.

Hans felt charges of electricity course through his arm and into his chest. He felt the lingering warmth of Clive's hand on his own. He hesitated before plunging into the water again, wishing that he could savor the caress a bit longer.

Each handover of a dish included a graze, a glance, a smile, a wink. Clive noticed an apron hung on a hook and grabbed it, wrapping it around his waist. Hans laughed and Clive placed his hand on his hip as if he were a woman protesting her domestic chores.

Clive took the stack of dishes and walked toward the pantry, where he placed them on a shelf. When he turned around, Hans was standing behind him with a large bowl. Rather than wait for Clive to move, Hans reached around him and set the bowl on the counter. They were face to face, and Clive could feel himself become aroused as Hans pressed against his crotch. Hans didn't move away. He pressed himself harder against Clive and leaned toward him, giving him a warm, moist kiss. Clive ran his hands over Hans' shoulder and pulled him close. He could feel Hans' heart beating against his own chest. Just as he was about to reach down and caress Hans' erection, Hans heard Margrit's steps as she returned from upstairs. He pulled Clive out of the pantry quickly and whispered, "She's coming."

Clive and Hans returned to their places in front of the sink, and Margrit peered from around the door and whispered, "*Er schläft.*"

Clive laid a serving spoon on the counter and walked toward Margrit. "*Einen After-Dinner-Drink für Sie?*" Clive had glanced around the kitchen and noticed a bottle of port. He took hold of it, held it up, and raised his brows.

Margrit nodded. Clive reached into a cupboard and removed a small glass, filling it with the dark amber liquid. "*Voilà, Frau Weber.*"

She chuckled. Hans glanced at their exchange and shook his head, his pulse still racing from the brief exchange earlier.

Margrit sat at the kitchen table. Hans looked at her as if to solicit her help with the dishes. "*Dir geht es ganz gut,*" she said, assuring him that he looked like he was doing just fine.

Clive brushed the back of his hand over his forehead as if perspiring from all the hard labor. "*Mein Gott!*"

They all laughed.

Hans and Clive finished washing the dishes and silverware.

"*Wollen wir ins Wohnzimmer gehen?*" Hans suggested.

Margrit and Clive looked at each other and nodded, walking toward the parlor.

Inside the cozy formal room, Hans threw some new logs onto the fire and offered everyone another pour of port. Margrit felt increasingly comfortable with Clive and wondered why he hadn't been snatched up. She found him exceedingly handsome – he had a broad forehead, deep brown eyes, and a sexy nose. Earlier comments about his athletic interests piqued her interest, and she began to undress him with her eyes, wondering what kind of physique his clothes concealed. She blushed and took a sip of port to hide her face.

"What kind of work do your parents do?" Hans asked.

Margrit edged forward in her chair to listen.

"My father is an engineer at a factory, and my mother is a teacher."

Margrit nodded as if she understood.

"So, will you follow in your father's footsteps?" Hans asked.

"God, no. I need something more intellectually stimulating."

"Like teaching or something?"

"I don't know – perhaps law. But with the war, I never felt like I had the luxury to imagine a future." Clive said pensively.

"But surely the war will end."

"But who will win? What will the world look like?"

Hans shook his head, imagining the worst. "If the war ended today, and Germany lost, what would you do?"

Clive rubbed his chin in thought and said, "I guess I'd have to say law. I'd like to represent people who are exploited and need representation — a public solicitor of sorts."

Margrit smiled. She grasped enough of what Clive said to realize he was compassionate, thoughtful, and intellectual – and she realized why Hans liked him, was drawn to him.

Clive glanced down at the coffee table and noticed some books. "What are you reading?" he asked Hans.

Hans looked over at Margrit and said, "They are Margrit's books. She's a voracious reader."

"*Was lesen Sie gerne?*" Clive asked about her interests.

Margrit was surprised Clive addressed her; was interested in what she thought, liked, did. Clive gazed at Margrit, waiting for her response.

"*Ich mag Romane. Zum Beispiel – diesen hier von Thomas Mann.*" She lifted a book by Thomas Mann and ran her hands over the cover.

Clive nodded, familiar with the increasing popularity of the author — popular in the German-speaking world. "*Mögen Sie Philosophie?*"

Margrit nodded no, that she didn't care that much for philosophy. But she added, "*Ich mag Romane mit philosophischen Themen.*"

Clive looked at Hans to translate. "Apparently, she likes love stories with philosophy mixed in."

Margrit blushed. Hans shook his head. Clive raised his brows, increasingly intrigued by the open-mindedness of Hans' wife.

They continued talking until the logs began to burn out and the port bottle was empty. Clive stood and began to take his leave, thanking them both for a memorable evening. Hans shook Clive's hand warmly, and Margrit bowed toward him. As the door closed behind him, Clive walked in the brisk night air back to the town center to join his comrades in the Princess Hotel.

He felt a warmth in his chest. The evening had been wonderful – a chance to get to know Hans in an entirely different setting. He had fully imagined Margrit to be a plain, uncomplicated, and subservient *Hausfrau*. To his surprise, she was clever, curious, and beautiful. He could see why Hans was drawn to her.

He chuckled to himself as he imagined the three of them in the kitchen – Hans sweating over the sink, Margrit standing her ground, and he wrapped in an apron, wiping his brow dramatically. They brought out his playful side, and he could fully imagine the three of them becoming close, very close. He wondered if Margrit could help Hans relax, could perhaps accept the affections between them, and, at some point, entertain some kind of arrangement.

15

⚜

Chapter Fifteen – Fragile Resolutions

Mürren November 1917

Hans leaned over his desk, reviewing files and planning the day. He scribbled notes on the charts of several soldiers who had made significant progress. Their TB symptoms had been negligible for weeks, and he would recommend a termination of their prescribed regime. He felt elated that the treatment had been successful and was eager to share the good news with them.

He felt unusually fatigued, having tossed and turned all night. Having hoped to reconcile the competing domains of his life, he had invited Clive to dinner. He hoped Clive might realize he was a happily married man. Perhaps he was trying to convince himself of the same thing. He wasn't sure what he hoped to achieve, except that he wasn't comfortable with how things were unfolding with Clive. The evening had gone better than he expected. Margrit didn't seem to suspect anything, even though she seemed unusually curious of their guest. And Clive had warmed to her. Hans had fully expected them to feel antipathy toward one another, but they seemed as if they had been long-time friends.

Nevertheless, sleep hadn't come easily. Each time he closed his eyes, his mind raced. He felt the warmth of Margrit's body lying next to him and the peaceful, almost imperceptible sound of each breath she took. Over the course of the evening, he realized how independent and clever she was, a woman who was well-read and capable of holding her own in conversation. He was both proud of her and unnerved by her sharp mind. The indiscretions with Clive weighed heavy on his conscience, and he hoped she wouldn't eventually sniff things out.

He tried to ignore Clive's distinctive scent still lingering in the house, the impressions Clive's affectionate touches had left as they did dishes together, and his imploring eyes, asking for far more than Hans was prepared to give. Hans' heart pounded in his chest. He needed to get his life under control. Rising several times during the night, and pacing the living room floor, he was determined to be a devoted husband, a loving father, and an ethical physician.

He returned to bed, inched close to Margrit, but his mind wouldn't be still. He rose again and again, drinking hot milk, sitting in the large chair near the glowing embers of the fireplace, and finally dosing off while reading a medical journal.

Margrit startled him around seven when she woke to feed Conrad. She looked at him quizzically, and he feared she knew. No, it wouldn't work. He couldn't maintain two parallel worlds. He had to find a way to distance himself from Clive. After eating breakfast and dressing, he walked along the snowy road to his office.

The mountain air was crisp, but the sky was clear, and the sun beat strongly on the south-facing terrace of the hotel. A nurse approached his office, knocked on the doorjamb, and announced that the prisoners were on their chaises and ready for examination. She noted that a few were presenting with new symptoms, but others seemed better. Hans compared the nurse's observations with his charts and then rose to make rounds.

As he walked onto the deck, he took a deep breath. The burden of caring for so many wounded men weighed heavily on him. These were young men at the prime of their lives fighting debilitating wounds, crippling respiratory ailments, and tuberculosis. He made his way down the row, avoiding eye contact with Clive who reclined on chaise eleven.

At patient eight, Albert, he glanced up and noticed Clive was reading. He took a deep breath, rehearsing in his mind how he might maintain a professional demeanor when he eventually arrived at his bed. Patients nine and ten – Rod and Paul – had done well. Their TB symptoms had dissipated, and Hans prescribed other therapies to improve lung capacity and physical strength. They dressed, shook Hans' hands warmly, and made their way off the terrace.

Clive glanced up as Hans turned toward him. Hans felt his legs grow weak and his heart race. It was impossible to ignore Clive's allure. He was seductive without even trying. His body was stretched out on the chaise, aglow in the sunlight. A book was propped against Clive's right leg, raised on the bed. Hans looked evasively at Clive's chart, busily scribbling notes.

"Doc, thanks for last night. Margrit is lovely, and Conrad is so cute. Thanks for being so generous in inviting me. I enjoyed the evening."

Hans looked over at the adjoining patients and feared they might overhear his conversation with Clive. He didn't want to appear to have favorites, and he certainly didn't want anyone to think something was going on between them. He said quickly, "Private Williams, can you come to my office after I finish rounds? I need to review some matters in your chart."

Clive raised his brows, wondering what might be behind the invitation. He nodded.

Hans continued, "Let me check your vitals."

Clive arched his back so that his chest stretched forward, ready for Hans's stethoscope. As he did so, the folds of his bed sheet slid down. Hans peered down at the dark shadows of Clive's undershorts, unable to peel his gaze away from the assets he knew lay within. Hans moved the stethoscope across Clive's chest, pressing here and there and listening as he took in deep breaths of air.

Hans placed his hand on Clive's warm shoulder and pressed him forward, running the bell of the device down his back. It took every ounce of self-control to resist an affectionate caress. He fought powerful competing urges. He wanted to get control over his errant desires and treat Clive like any other patient. It was an urgent matter. His family and livelihood depended on his professional behavior.

But Clive was handsome, smart, clever, witty, and affable. Hans could feel himself lose control, as if swept by a vortex, drawing him deeper and deeper into Clive's aura. It was as if Clive's beauty — physical and personal — could be possessed and made his own. He had merely to hold him, touch him, breathe him in. It was an irresistible urge, one that promised his own wholeness and vitality, as if by becoming one with Clive he would connect with himself.

"I'll see you later," Hans said to Clive as he made notes on the chart.

Clive nodded, and Hans moved to the next patient.

After lunch, Clive dressed and walked to Hans' office. He knocked on the door and pressed it open. Uncharacteristically,

Hans was seated in a chair in front of the desk near the fireplace. He stood and motioned for Clive to sit in the adjacent chair.

"Some brandy?" Hans offered.

"What's the occasion?" Clive inquired with suspicion.

"Nothing special." In reality, he was hoping to calm his nerves. He stood and poured them both a drink, handing an amber-filled class to Clive. They clinked glasses, and each took a sip.

"I enjoyed last night," Clive began.

"Yes. It was delightful. Margrit found you quite charming."

"She's a special woman."

"Hmm," Hans murmured. "Yes. I'm very fortunate. I love her dearly."

Clive peered curiously at Hans, taking another sip of his drink. He surmised Hans was nervous and preoccupied. "How does it work?" Clive asked.

"What?"

"This."

"This what?"

"You know. Us and her," Clive stated.

"I don't know what you mean," Hans said, taking a long sip of the brandy. His face turned red.

"Doc. You are married yet you and I – you know."

Hans squirmed in his chair and cleared his throat. "That's just friendly affection. Nothing more."

Clive raised his brows in surprise. "I'm pretty sure it's more than what two friends share with one another."

"Let's not talk about that. I just wanted to have a friendly conversation with you. I noticed you were reading a book on Plato."

"Actually, I was reading one of his dialogues."

"Which one?" Hans inquired.

Clive rolled his eyes. Hans' questions were always a prelude to something else. Yes, they shared interests in philosophy, history, politics, and other topics, but the discussions all ended in the same place, in each other's arms. "I'm reading *Phaedrus*."

Hans looked quizzically at Clive, unfamiliar with the book.

"It's one of Plato's dialogues on the soul and love."

Hans stared at Clive apprehensively. "What does it say?"

"There's a lot in it, and there's a lot of controversy about what Plato intended. Parts of the dialogue discuss the immortality of the soul and reincarnation. Other sections are about love."

Hans continued to stare at Clive, encouraging him to continue.

"The part I find intriguing is Plato's notion of madness."

"What do you mean?"

"Plato seems to suggest that while reason and logic are important for virtue and the right conduct of the soul, so, too, is madness or a sort of loss of reason and logic. There's a sense in which some practices – like prophecy, poetry, and mysticism require a divine inspiration that seizes us when we have let go of rational control.

"And what does that have to do with love?"

"Plato suggests that true love ideally seeks the well-being of the beloved. There's a sense in which the relationship between a man and someone who is not his beloved is a safer relationship, a more noble relationship, since there is no passion that might cloud reason or judgment. But Plato says in other instances, the god Eros guides a lover to the beloved. He suggests that there can be something good, providential, benign in sexual attraction. It is as if madness or eros leads two people together so that they come to recognize and affirm the good and beautiful in each other."

Hans wiped his forehead. He had begun to perspire. He felt the madness, the uncontrolled passion for Clive. But it couldn't be good. It clouded his reason and judgment. Evasively, to change the subject, he asked, "What does he say about the immortality of the soul?"

Clive raised his brows, cognizant of Hans' evasive question. "The soul is immaterial and doesn't die. It takes many lifetimes to develop wings capable of ascending to higher realms, such as the realm of the gods or even higher dominions. For philosophers, the number of lifetimes required to achieve that is less. For others, it is longer."

"So, we have lived before?"

"That's what Plato says. If you think about it, some people possess a sort of genius that isn't traceable to their own life experiences. There are times we sense a familiarity with a place or a person that is inexplicable given our current lifetime."

"I'm not sure I believe in that," Hans said matter-of-factly.

Clive sensed that his and Hans' meeting had been fated, as if destiny had brought them together, two souls who had perhaps known each other in another lifetime and had unfinished business. The sequence of events that had led him to Mürren and to Hans was too improbable not to be providential, not to have been guided by some force or past connection. He was certain the attraction he felt for Hans and that Hans felt for him was more than mere lust. It was purposeful and full of opportunity for personal transformation and enrichment. Given Hans' state of mind, he wasn't sure he could be successful in explaining his thoughts to him now.

To calm Hans down, he said, "I have to read more to figure it out."

Hans sighed deeply.

"More brandy?" Hans asked as he lifted the bottle toward Clive's glass.

Clive nodded.

Hans poured them each a second glass. He then said, "Last night you mentioned interest in perhaps becoming a lawyer."

"Hmm. Yes. I've been thinking about that," Clive noted.

"And why?"

"To represent those who don't have representation. There are too many people who lack resources to deal with situations they didn't create. I'd like to help."

"That's very admirable. You're a clever man, and I'm sure you would do well in that field."

"I just don't know what will happen after the war, if it ever ends."

"It must end, and Germany will be vanquished."

"I hope you are right."

"You have an active intellect and curiosity. You have a passion for justice. That's rare to find these days."

Clive blushed. "I don't know if that is enough."

"It's a good start. How many of your colleagues read like you do or contemplate philosophical, political or even social justice kinds of questions?"

Clive murmured, "Hmm." He shook his head as if to convey incertitude.

"You should pursue your dreams," Hans stated.

"We'll see what happens. In the meantime, I am grateful for your care, our friendship, and the opportunity to ski and hike these magnificent mountains."

Hans was relieved Clive used the term friendship rather than love. He took a deep breath. But, as he did, he couldn't help gazing into Clive's dark, alluring eyes. They were filled with wonder, idealism, and mystery. Clive's dark, wavy hair seemed exceptionally soft and silky in the orange glow of the fire. He wanted to run his hands through it. Recalling Plato's use of the term madness, he trembled. He felt it. His body and its inclinations had a mind of their own, drawing him inexorably toward this handsome man in front of him. His desires defied all sense of decorum, reason, and convention. He took a long sip of his brandy, hoping to quell the errant longing he felt deep within.

Hans stood and began to pace back and forth in front of the fireplace.

"What's wrong?" Clive asked.

"Nothing," Hans replied, lying.

Clive stood and walked toward Hans. He placed a hand on Hans' shoulder. Hans melted at the warmth and strength in Clive's palm. "It must be difficult," Clive remarked without specification.

A tear formed in Hans' eye. Clive stood back, giving Hans space. Hans didn't want space. He wanted to be held by the one man who understood him. Hans gave Clive an imploring look. Clive approached and embraced him.

Hans felt safe and cherished in Clive's powerful arms. Clive's formidable body conveyed resilience and strength, virtues Hans wished he had more of. He gazed into Clive's eyes and remarked on how tender and playful they were.

"How do you do it?" Hans inquired of Clive.

"What?"

"You're so calm, strong, and clear-headed. Yet you are a prisoner in a foreign country away from your family."

"I derive a lot of strength from you," Clive remarked, gazing tenderly into Hans' eyes. "I don't know what I would do without you."

Hans felt his heart skip a beat. Clive's words were both heartening and frightening. He placed his hands on Clive's chest, one that had been weakened underneath by TB but which, nevertheless, was broad and firm. He could feel the warmth underneath

Clive's shirt. Trembling, he slipped his fingers in between the buttons and felt his warm skin.

Clive felt himself become aroused. The closeness of Hans' body, the warmth of his hand, and the sweet smell of brandy on his breath were intoxicating. Hans' resolve was thawing. Clive ran his hand down the small of Hans' back and over the top of his buttocks. As he pulled Hans close, he could feel his desire pressed against him.

Without hesitation, Hans reached down and unbuttoned Clive's trousers. He reached in and felt the warm contours of Clive's flesh. It was madness — a frenzy of craving that took hold of him. He needed Clive. Clive made him feel young, manly, strong, smart, and handsome.

Clive cocked his head back and let Hans hold him. He wanted Hans to want him, to love him.

With Clive in his hand, Hans gazed at his face. His eyes were closed, and the crimson hue of his skin had become aflame. Clive's broad forehead and deeply set eyes suggested someone of deep thought and intelligence. Clive was beautiful. Clive was good. Could Clive be right? Could the frenzy of his craving be a way that the gods drew him to someone so noble and wonderful?

Hans felt his own heart race as he felt Clive's building pleasure ready to explode. Awkwardly, he unbuttoned his own trousers and let them fall to the floor. Clive opened his eyes and took hold of Hans. He leaned over and surrounded Hans' sexy, moist mouth with his own. He breathed Hans in – this caring and tender doctor who had been a safe port during a tumultuous war. Hans' body was home. It was warmth, potency, intellect, and companionship.

Clive pressed Hans toward one of the chairs in front of the fireplace. He nudged him back into the chair and kneeled between his legs. Hans tugged at Clive's shirt and felt the buttons pop open.

He slid the fabric off Clive's shoulders and ran his hands through his hair and over his round, muscular shoulders. He could feel the warmth and wetness of Clive's mouth on him. He lost all sense of time and place, riding the waves of pleasure coursing through his body.

Clive wanted Hans to feel his love and affection, to know he loved him more than any other. He wanted Hans' apprehension to subside, to give way to an appreciation for how two men could love each other, not just as friends but as lovers, each craving union with the other.

Clive ran his hand up under Hans' shirt and felt the contours of his abdomen and chest. He caressed him with abandon, pressing hard on the muscles and skin to break apart any latent barrier or armor Hans had erected. Hans gave himself over to Clive's hands and mouth, allowing himself to be taken, to be consumed. Soon, he came with a forceful climax and collapsed in the chair.

Clive lingered and caressed Hans' thighs. He lifted his head and gave Hans a warm smile.

Hans felt his heart return to normal, and his breathing slowed.

Clive laid his head on Hans' leg. Hans hesitatingly brushed his hand through Clive's hair. Clive could feel his hesitation and braced himself for Hans' remorse. Eventually, Clive rose, pulled up his trousers and buttoned his shirt. Hans did the same.

There was a heavy silence in the room, broken only by the crackle of wood in the fireplace.

Hans said, "I'm sorry."

Clive shook his head. "Don't be."

Hans shook his head. "I was resolved to be better. I failed."

Armed with Plato's insights, Clive said, "You are a beautiful man, Hans. You are a devoted husband and loving father. You and

I have a special relationship that is good for each of us. There is nothing to be ashamed of. You have a big heart."

Hans' head hung low. His heart didn't feel big. He felt that everyone he loved he betrayed — Margrit, Conrad, and even Clive. Yes, he loved Clive, but he couldn't give him his heart. He would be lost if he did. There was no road map for that, nor for the wilderness he found himself traversing. An all-too-familiar war raged inside him. Contradictions loomed large and insurmountable. He sighed deeply, unable to find his way out of the quagmire of self-hate and shame.

"I have to go," Hans said to Clive, glancing at his watch. "I'll see you around?" he added.

Clive nodded. He touched Hans affectionately on his upper arm and smiled. "It will be okay."

Hans stared at Clive as if he hadn't heard the words. Clive turned and left the office.

16

Chapter Sixteen – Awkward

Mürren Winter 2007

At breakfast the next morning, Sofia approached Elliott's table to offer him coffee. She gasped for breath as she stood over him. Elliott had dark circles under his eyes, and he looked pale, ashen.

"Coffee?"

"Hm hmm," Elliott murmured without elaboration or pleasantries.

Sofia poured him a cup. She hesitated, then asked, "Are you okay?"

"Hmm. Yes," Elliott replied unconvincingly, trying to conserve energy.

"Did Max push you too hard yesterday?"

Elliott took an evasive sip of coffee, unnerved at Sofia's presumably innocent yet precise question.

"He has a tendency to do that. He is always trying to prove himself," she added.

Elliott began to perspire. Her follow-up remarks made him wonder if Sofia was ignorant of what had transpired, or clever and sadistic. He looked up to see if he could detect something in her face.

She grinned, as if she held a secret. Elliott said, "Max is an excellent skier. I may have pushed myself too hard."

"Well, take your time this morning. We don't have a full house, and I'm not in a rush to clear the breakfast tables."

"You're very kind. Thanks."

Elliott slowly sipped the coffee and glanced out of the large window at the surrounding mountains. It was a sunny day, and it would be nice to ski. But he thought it might be good to take it easy, perhaps do some snowshoeing or hiking. He had tossed and turned all night, fighting a war within himself – glee at having had a deeply satisfying romp with Max and guilt for violating his and Sofia's relationship.

He was also troubled by Max's abrupt departure. He wasn't sure what had precipitated his hasty exit – was it guilt, shame, or something that the photo of his great grandfather triggered? Max was absent from the breakfast crew, and that unnerved him even more.

After slowly consuming some muesli and a few rolls with butter and marmalade, Elliott pushed his chair back and began to stand. The dining room had emptied earlier, everyone eager to take advantage of the splendid conditions and good weather. Sofia approached. "Another cup of coffee?" she asked, holding a pot of coffee over his cup and pressing down on his shoulder, keeping him from rising.

Elliott hesitated, glanced at the cup, and peered into Sofia's eyes – curious, stern, and commanding. Guilt washed over him as the reality of what he and Max had done sunk in. While he hadn't initiated their exchange, he had done nothing to stop it.

"Do you have a minute?" she asked.

Elliott turned red. He nodded apprehensively and eased back in his chair. Sofia poured coffee into his cup and into the one she had in her hand.

"It's not often I have a moment like this," she added as she pulled a chair from a nearby table and sat facing Elliott.

He felt his stomach tighten, wondering if she was softening him up for the kill.

"So, you had a good day on the slopes yesterday?" she continued.

"Yes," Elliott replied, not sure how much Max had shared with her.

"Max seemed to have enjoyed himself," she said stoically, as if he wasn't supposed to.

Elliott raised his brows and said, "I hope I didn't hold him back."

"No. I don't think that was the case. He seemed like he was quite tired this morning. What is it you say in English - you gave him a run for his money?"

Elliott felt his heart pound, unnerved at Sofia's remark.

"Did he sleep in?"

"No. He's been in the cellar sorting through a new delivery of food and beverages. But he seems to be moving slower than usual."

Elliott took an evasive sip of his coffee. He said, "We did quite a few runs. But he must be used to it."

"He can't put out like he used to."

Elliott raised his brows. He hoped Sofia's statement stemmed from her limited English vocabulary and wasn't a not-so-subtle allusion. "Do you mean he can't do as much as he used to?"

"Oh, yes. Sorry for my English." She chuckled.

"I'm sure it is a lot of tiring work running an inn."

Sofia nodded. "It's never ending."

"Do you ever get a vacation?"

"We usually close in November and April. But we often stay here. There are repairs to make."

"What do you do in your free time? Do you ski, too?"

"Not anymore. My knees are bad."

"Sorry to hear. So, what do you do when you have a day off?"

"I have friends in Wengen. We meet up for lunch or drinks."

"What about Max?"

"Oh, my friends are all women. He doesn't come."

"What does he do in free time?"

"He skis or hikes."

"With friends?"

"Mostly by himself."

"What's it like living in Mürren? Is there a nice community here?"

Sofia nodded yes, but her face was sullen. "But many of our friends have children and don't have time to socialize."

Elliott felt sadness for Sofia and Max and wondered if life in Mürren wasn't terribly lonely – even with all the tourists coming and going. The thought sparked an observation. "You must make friends with your guests."

Sofia twitched. She looked off evasively. She turned back to Elliott and said, "It's not often that we have time to sit like this and visit with a guest. Either we are busy, or they are occupied with their kids."

"I know. I'm an odd guest," Elliott noted, scrutinizing Sofia, trying to make sense of her friendly words but cold body language.

She grinned. He was unusual, and Max seemed both off-put and fascinated with him. She was curious why.

"Well, you're free."

Elliott gave her a quizzical look.

"You can sit and talk over coffee or have a brandy after dinner. Not like our other guests."

Elliott wondered if that was a good or bad thing and said, "I'm sorry. I hope I'm not keeping you from your work."

"It's not a problem," she said, glancing into Elliott's dark brown eyes. They were mesmerizing, and she felt a stirring in her chest. Elliott was handsome. "Some things are more important than work."

Elliott felt himself become flush. He felt the intensity of Sofia's regard and worried she might have feelings for him, too. He couldn't tell if she was interrogating him about Max or feeling him out. He chuckled nervously to himself.

The information Sofia had discovered about Hans and Clive still troubled her. She asked, "When you were younger, did your grandfather talk about his time here?"

"No. As I mentioned before, he seemed reluctant, troubled, sad." Elliott was relieved the topic had shifted.

"No stories about Margrit or Hans?"

"I only saw a reference to Margrit on the postcard I showed you when I was a teenager. After Clive died, I found other cards and decided to make a visit. I've been curious about his time here. I never realized there was a personal connection to the inn."

Sofia was restless. Her legs shook under the table. "Your grandfather never talked about Hans?" she asked pointedly.

"No," Elliott said without elaboration, wondering why Sofia asked about him and not Margrit.

Sofia didn't know how to frame her follow up question. She was curious about male companionship, even the possibility of romantic affection between them. But she had never given expressions to those curiosities before. "Did your grandfather keep in touch with his comrades from the war?"

"I don't know. I don't think so. But he came to Grindelwald often."

"Hmm," Sofia murmured. "Did he have close friends here?"

Elliott looked off into the distance as if in thought. He turned back to Sofia and said, "When I used to come with him, he had a lot of friends. Everyone seemed to know him."

"Men or women?"

"Why do you ask?"

"Just curious," she said, blushing.

"Both." But as Elliott answered the question, the images of his grandfather interacting with people in Grindelwald were, for the most part, images of camaraderie with men, handsome men, affectionate men.

Sofia looked out of the window as if distracted. She pivoted back toward Elliott and said, "Well, I think I should let you relax. I also have chores to do."

Elliott looked at her curiously. It seemed like an abrupt end to the conversation.

"One last question," Sofia interjected as she slid her chair back from the table. "Why is a handsome man like you single?"

Oh shit, Elliott thought to himself. She knows. "Hmm," he began timidly, blushing. "I guess bad luck."

"Haven't met the right person yet?" she pressed.

Sofia's gender-neutral question impressed him. He thought to himself, she's smooth. She's zeroing in for the kill.

"As I'm sure you've noticed, I'm rather fussy. I think it would be difficult for someone to warm up to me and manage all of my idiosyncrasies."

"Oh, that's just your defensive shield. I detect, under the surface, you are quite capable of sweeping someone off their feet." She winked at him.

Elliott turned red. He lifted his cup to take a sip to avoid eye contact with Sofia. The cup was empty. She grinned at him as if she detected his discomfort.

He hoped she was flirting with him and not making an allusion to him and Max. He would be horrified if she knew and if she had been playing with him all along.

"You're too kind," he replied.

She glared at him without emotion.

He was still uncertain of her agenda.

17

Chapter Seventeen – Shame

Murren Winter 2007

Elliott realized he needed an easier agenda after the aggressive ski day with Max. He thought he might do some snowshoeing. The inn had some shoes guests could use, and there was easy access to a network of paths that stretched away from town. The trails wound their way downhill, where a charming lodge served stew to skiers and hikers with stunning views of the surrounding mountains.

Elliott found the walk a perfect antidote to the surprising events of the night before, a chance to reflect and ponder what had transpired with Max. The image of Max's abrupt departure only reinforced Elliott's resolve to cool things, having undoubtedly pushed Max beyond his comfort zone, even if it had been Max who had made the overture. He wasn't sure how things would unfold in such an intimate inn, where he would have to interact with Max over the next ten days. He wondered if he should check out and return to England.

On his way back from his walk, as Elliott climbed the steep hill toward the inn, he noticed Max was chopping firewood near a shed behind the building. It would be impossible to avoid him, so he continued his trek forward. His breathing became laborious, and he wondered if it was from the strenuous exercise or the anxiousness about what he would say when he crossed paths with Max.

Max waved at him in a way that suggested he was busy and hoped Elliott would continue on his way. But Elliott felt compelled to stop, to confront things, and to clear the air. He walked toward Max, who set his ax down and took a long sip of water.

"Hello," Max said, nodding to Elliott. Apprehension filled his eyes. "Did you have a pleasant walk?"

"It was beautiful, although I feel out of shape!"

"The mountains are unforgiving."

"Hmm," Elliott murmured, hoping the comment was not a foreshadowing. He gazed into Max's eyes, trying to take a read.

Max extended his hand with a bottle of water, offering it to Elliott. Elliott said, "*Danke schön,*" and took a long sip.

Restless, Max cleared his throat. He said quietly, "I'm terribly sorry."

"There's nothing to apologize for. If anything, I should apologize to you."

Max gave him a quizzical look.

Elliott continued, "I'm sure you get all sorts of people here who make overtures. You're handsome, warm, friendly, and accommodating. People will take advantage of your hospitality."

Max looked off evasively. In fact, he had been the object of several overtures over the years, particularly when he was younger. The pattern was not all that imaginative. A guest would report a problem, Max would go to the room to fix it, and the guest would make advances.

Some guests were more handsome than others. The unattractive ones were easy to manage. When someone made a pass, Max would calmly say, "I forgot a tool. Or I have to go get some supplies." He left and never returned. Rarely did anyone bring things up later.

The handsome ones were another matter. When new guests arrived, Max could tell immediately who would make an overture. There was something in their gaze that gave them away. He could feel them follow him with their eyes as he served dinner or catch them staring at him when he had been otherwise busy. Over the years, he had learned how to resist their advances, some more easily than others.

Elliott had been the first guest with whom he had lost control, and it bothered him terribly. Elliott was annoying and peculiar, but he made Max's legs go weak and his pulse race. There was something in his expressive eyes, his luscious lips, and his sexy nose that he found irresistible. When he served him at dinner or prepared a brandy for him in the parlor, he felt his skin become flush and his heart pound. He kept berating himself for his thoughts, and hoped he might remain firm in his resolve to behave professionally, but then Sofia had to ruin things by committing him to a ski day with Elliott.

As the day on the slopes progressed, his attraction to Elliott increased, and he found it increasingly difficult to deny his feelings. He felt like a giddy teenager, inviting Elliott for a drink in the parlor. He hoped Elliott might not have the same feelings and would have provided a guard rail to Max's ravenous inclinations. He felt as if he had been possessed when he asked to see Elliott's postcards in his room, and he felt even more out of control when Elliott turned and peered at him with his dark, alluring eyes.

"Why should you apologize? I'm the innkeeper. I shouldn't be taking advantage of guests."

Elliott resisted stating the obvious. Max shared a business and life with Sofia. He had violated the trust between them. Elliott felt horrible and wondered if Max didn't feel terribly guilty – not so much for coming on to a guest, but for betraying Sofia.

"Last night you seemed unnerved when you saw the photograph of my grandfather and your great grandfather. What was it that triggered such a strong reaction? Was it the love of two men?"

"I don't want to talk about it."'

"We need to talk about it. It's important to clear the air."

Max turned away from him and picked up the ax, positioning it over a log he intended to split.

"Max?"

"I don't know," he said, evading Elliott's eyes.

"Are you gay? Does that trouble you?"

Max began to tremble, and his eyes turned red. He laid the ax back down as if defeated. Glancing out over the snow field behind the inn, Max began to sob.

Elliott wasn't sure what to do. He unfastened his snowshoes and approached Max. He put one of his hands on Max's shoulder. He could feel him shaking. His skin was warm and moist under the flannel shirt he wore.

"It's okay. It's never easy to come out," Elliott said. He couldn't imagine what it would be like in a small alpine village where everyone knew everything about everyone. He imagined the news would be devastating for Sofia and upend her life.

"*Es ist nicht das*," Max said, denying that the issue was about being gay.

Elliott turned Max toward him and gave him a curious look.

Max continued to shake, and Elliott wanted to embrace him but held back.

"*Es war Georg*."

"Your great grandfather's brother?"

Max nodded. Then he continued. "Niklaus."

"Who is Niklaus?"

"*Der Bruder meines Grossvaters.*"

Elliott peered into Max's hazel eyes, searching for more information, not sure he understood the German. They were sullen and filled with tears.

"My grandfather's brother," Max clarified.

"And?"

Max turned ashen. He looked like he was about to faint. Elliott took hold of the back of his elbow and supported him.

Max shook his head no. "I can't."

"You can't what?"

"I can't say it."

Elliott realized there was something profound that Max needed to get off his chest. He nodded to him encouragingly. "Tell me."

Max hesitated. He looked off evasively, pensively. Quietly, he said, "When I saw the photograph of Georg, I had a bad reaction."

"Why?"

"He looks like Niklaus."

"It's curious how people in a particular family tree resemble each other," Elliott observed.

"It provoked a painful memory, particularly after what we had just done."

Elliott gulped. He knew what Max was about to say. He wanted to hold him and quell the trembling, but knew Max needed to let it go.

"*Ich wurde missbraucht. Sexuell.*"

Elliott wasn't familiar with the words Max had spoken, but it was clear what he had said, what he was trying to disclose. Max had been sexually abused. "Oh Max. How horrible. I'm sorry. How old were you?"

"Sixteen."

"By your great uncle?"

"Hm hmm." Tears streaked down his cheeks.

"Did you ever report it?"

"You're the first person I've ever told," he said, quivering.

"You're kidding. You've been holding it in all these years?"

Max nodded.

"Oh my God."

"I'm a mess. Such a fuckup."

"Max. It's not your fault."

"I'm a bad person."

"Your great uncle is a bad person. He should have never done that to you."

Max couldn't shake the terrifying thoughts – the stale odor of cigarettes and whiskey on his great uncle's breath, the roughness of his unshaven beard rubbing against his face, and the pain he felt days after – one that was both physical and emotional. He felt shame for having taken hold of himself while his great uncle penetrated him. He had jerked hard, feeling pulsations of pleasure mixed with an intense ache that filled his body. He hated it and he craved it. The contradiction had tortured him his whole life.

Elliott felt Max's sense of disgrace, one he had seen too often in his friends – male and female. Elliott knew that what transpired between Max's great uncle and him was shameful, and too often the victim internalized the shame, a shame wrapped in sex. For gay men who were abused by men, it was difficult to accept their orientation without equating it with something clandestine, dark, and abusive.

"I should have never done what I did to you," Max said to Elliott.

"We both did what we did freely."

"But you were vulnerable. You are a guest."

Elliott was amazed Max had put his finger on the relevant issue about abuse, the betrayal of someone's vulnerability. But in his and Max's case, that really wasn't the issue. There was no betrayal or force. "We are all vulnerable. We wonder if someone will love us as we are. We expose our insecurities as we let another touch us."

Max began to shake again. It was clear that he felt vulnerable and exposed and unsafe. "I have to go," he said suddenly to Elliott.

"Let's talk."

"I can't."

Elliott rubbed his hand over Max's shoulder, and Max shrugged it off. He didn't want to be touched. He didn't want to be loved. He didn't want to be vulnerable. He couldn't; it only reminded him of what Niklaus had done.

"Max, I'm here for you if you want to talk."

Max turned away from Elliott and raised his hand toward him as if to say, 'back away.' He didn't want to talk.

"Are you okay?"

Max nodded. "I'll see you later."

Elliott gazed at him to take a read. Max was in pain, but he needed solitude. He picked up his snowshoes, placed them under his arms, and walked to the main entrance of the inn.

Later that evening, Elliott took his seat in the dining room as guests arrived and staff served drinks and appetizers. He glanced around the room. Sofia nodded to him from the kitchen door, but Max was nowhere to be seen.

Sofia brought a bowl of soup to Elliott, and he asked, "Where's Max? I hope he is okay."

She looked worried and said, "He's ill. He seems to have some kind of stomach virus. He's rarely sick, so whatever it is, it must be significant."

"I'm sorry to hear. I hope it isn't a delayed reaction to a tough day on the slopes."

"No. He's usually able to handle that. He complained of cramps in his stomach. Hopefully, it will pass."

"Give him my regards."

"I will."

18

Chapter Eighteen – Déjà vu

Grindelwald Winter 2007

The next day, Max wasn't at breakfast. Elliott was unnerved but unable to solicit any additional information from Sofia. She had put on her best innkeeper face and was, as usual, friendly and solicitous of her guests' needs.

Elliott had planned all week to go to Grindelwald to ski. It has been several years since his last trip. After breakfast, he returned to his room, slipping on his thermal underwear, ski socks, ski pants, boots, sweater, and jacket. He realized as he aged, the ordeal of dressing for the slopes became more challenging and cumbersome, but it was worth the effort.

He walked downstairs, retrieved his skis, and walked to the station. The train took him to Grütschalp where he took a cable car to Lauterbrunnen. There he took a train to Wengen. where he walked to the Männlichen lift. He recalled his first ride on the lift with his grandfather forty-five years earlier. At the top of the mountain, he took a deep breath and surveyed the stunning views of the Eiger and the more distant peak of the Wetterhorn across from the sunbathed slopes of First, on the other side of Grindelwald.

All morning, he felt as if Clive were present, sitting next to him on the train and now gazing out at the beautiful trails spread out before him. He recalled how aggressive a skier Clive was and knew which run he would have taken first. Elliott pivoted and pointed his skis toward one of the expert trails and made a series of well-controlled turns on the steep slope. He heard his grandfather's voice coach him as he made his way down the mountain.

It was an invigorating day. He had regained his ski legs and was enjoying the perfect conditions. By three, he was reaching his limits and skied down to Grindelwald, taking the train for a short ride from Grund to the main station where he rested his skis on a rack and walked into town. The village was teeming with tourists and skiers who were making their way to bars and cafes to enjoy après-ski drinks and appetizers.

Dorfstrasse looked as it always had – a pleasant roadway lined with ski shops, cafes, restaurants, hotels, and gift shops. Elliott made his way to a favorite hangout, a bar popular with the international crowd, one he used to patronize when Clive napped before dinner.

Pushing the door open, he felt the energy of the space – the lively music and the hum of conversations in a variety of languages. He made his way to the bar and found an empty seat with a great view of the room. He ordered a beer and nodded to those seated near him.

Skiing had helped him clear his head and put things into perspective. He realized he hadn't thought much about Max during the day and had been able to create a healthy distance. He realized that he didn't need to solve Max's problems.

Glancing around the room, one filled with people considerably younger than he was, Elliott realized he was close to being the creepy old man in the corner and almost left. For old times' sake, he remained and observed the crowd, reminiscing about earlier visits. He watched the young people, more comfortable with casual touch than he had been when he first came to the bar as an eighteen-year-old.

He watched a group of ski instructors in their bright red ski suits huddled together, drinking beers. They were celebrating the end of the workday, bantering back and forth and nudging each other playfully. He found it intriguing, even a bit arousing, that several of the male instructors had their arms wrapped over the shoulders of each other. He would have chalked it up to intoxicated male camaraderie, and there was clearly some of that, but two of them leaned toward each other at one point and kissed each other on the lips.

The others didn't blink an eye, carrying on as if their friends' affection was unremarkable. Elliott realized how fortunate they were to grow up in the world they did, and how long and tortuous the journey had been for his own self-acceptance.

He watched two other men at the far end of the bar who were chatting. They were young, perhaps still teens. They were sitting very close to each other, and there was an intensity in their eyes and gestures as they visited. The image of them stirred a memory, one that Elliott hadn't considered for quite some time. He remembered being their age, a time of wonder and self-discovery. He recalled being at a crossroads in his life, trying to figure out who he was and what he wanted out of life and love.

He watched the two guys at the end of the bar. They were young and handsome, just like he had been. One of them placed his hand on the other's thigh, and Elliott felt himself clinch his stomach. He thought it odd, a visceral reaction to male affection. He thought he had gotten over the negative tapes in his head and could celebrate being a gay man, but the image of those teens testing the waters and making awkward attempts at connecting with each other stirred troubling memories. He continued to watch them and felt his own discomfort grow. One of them stood, ready to leave. Elliott fully expected him to express disdain for the other's touch, perhaps glaring at him or raising his fist. He didn't. He leaned toward his companion and gave him a warm kiss. The other reached over and took his hand and held it as long as he could. As the one leaving reached the door, he looked back and winked at the other.

A tear streaked down Elliott's cheek. He realized that many years ago, if the guy he had met at the same bar had reacted differently to his casual gesture of camaraderie, he might not have made so many mistakes – marrying his wife and going through a string of failed relationships as he played tapes of rejection and shame over and over in his head. He wondered what would have happened if the guy he met had reciprocated Elliott's gesture or if the two of them had reconnected later that week or kept in touch. He struggled to recall the guy's name – was it Alex or Sebastian or something like that? He tried to visualize his face, but all that came to his mind was his clenched fist and the terror in his eyes.

Elliott glanced at his watch and realized it was time to go back to the inn. He walked to the station, hopped on board the train to Zweilütschinen, and from there made a series of connections, arriving in Mürren on the last train. He walked briskly to the inn, dropped his skis inside the front door, and proceeded quickly to the dining room, where dinner was in progress.

Sofia gave him a curious look as he took his seat. She came to his table and served him soup. "I was wondering where you were and if you had gotten into trouble someplace."

"Sorry. I skied to Grindelwald, had some drinks, and only managed to catch the last train back. I'm sorry if I gave you a fright."

"No problem," she said, although she seemed frazzled. She retreated to the kitchen, where she retrieved platters of cutlets she served to other guests.

Another server came and took Elliott's drink order, returning with a quarter liter of red wine. Elliott felt lost without his book and fussed nervously with silverware and the small vase of flowers on the table. He glanced around, looking for Max.

Suddenly, Max walked through the kitchen door with a platter of roasted vegetables. When he saw Elliott, he gasped for air. He had fully expected Elliott to have gone out to eat at another hotel, to avoid him, to avoid the tension between them. He almost dropped the platter but caught himself. He proceeded to several tables along the wall, doing what he could to avoid catching Elliott's eye.

He realized that to serve the last couple of tables, he would have to walk past Elliott's table. He felt his legs grow weak and his pulse race. His heart pounded, uncertain about what to say or how to react when their eyes eventually crossed.

Elliott looked over and noticed Max. He was relieved that Max was no longer ill, but apprehensive about how he might react. Max looked up and caught Elliott's eyes. Elliott looked exceedingly handsome. He had on a sporty ski sweater and form-fitting ski pants, not his usual dinner outfit. His hair was tousled, and his skin was still rosy from the cold air outside.

Elliott nodded to Max and, as he did, he had a déjà vu. They were the same eyes, the same round face, and the same sexy nose. He glanced at Max's shoulders, ones he had touched playfully, affectionately decades earlier. He realized he had met Max before, and he felt himself grow faint, taking hold of the side of the table to brace himself as his head spun.

Max approached Elliott's table and felt his own stomach tighten. He glanced at Elliott's soup bowl and, without looking him in the eye, asked if he could take it in preparation for the main course. Elliott nodded almost imperceptibly.

Elliott felt dizzy and ate a piece of bread, hoping to regain composure. He took a long sip of water and began to calculate in his head when he must have first met Max. It was roughly thirty-seven years ago when he had been in Grindelwald with his grandfather. He realized it would have been about the time Max had been abused by his great uncle, thus explaining his frightening reaction to Elliott's casual and friendly gesture of affection. He shook his head in amazement, wondering how the fates could have orchestrated such a reunion. It was as if time had bent backwards to bring them together.

Sofia returned with Elliott's main course. "All good?" she asked as she placed his dinner on the table. She noticed his face was red and his forehead moist.

"Hmm," Elliott said, nodding. Before she left, he interjected, "It looks like Max is feeling better."

"Yes. Although he's still not himself."

"Some things take a long time to get over," he said pointedly, unsure what to do with the information circling in his head.

"So, you had a good day?" she asked.

"Yes. I had a chance to reminisce about old times with my grandfather."

"That's nice," Sofia said without much emotion, moving on to several other tables she was serving.

Elliott felt as if both Sofia and Max were being friendly, but more formal than usual. He felt increasingly ill at ease. He rapidly consumed his meal. Sofia passed several times, but Max seemed to have disappeared.

When he finished dinner, he walked toward the kitchen and gingerly pressed the door open. Max was busy arranging platters he had cleaned. He glanced over to Elliott. He felt a flutter in his stomach. He tried to shake the images that flashed in his head - Elliott's warm skin gliding over his own and the feel of Elliott's hardness in his hand.

"The dinner was delicious," he began, hoping to engage Max.

"Thanks. Glad you enjoyed it," Max replied without looking Elliott in the eyes. He continued to organize platters on the counter.

Sofia could feel the tension between them. She didn't know what altercation they must have had, but she didn't want to get in the middle of it. She left and went to the office.

Elliott peered at Max, taking a protracted look at his eyes, his nose, his mouth. He was certain Max was the young man he met many years ago. "Max, are you okay?"

"Fine," he said unconvincingly.

"Can we talk?"

"There's nothing to talk about. I'm sorry."

"So am I," Elliott said. As he voiced his apology, the memory of standing before Max as a teenager intensified. He recalled the same bewilderment he felt years before. But now he knew the reason for Max's stern demeanor. When he was eighteen, he thought he had done something wrong, something to provoke his new chum. And while guilt now coursed through his veins, particularly as Sofia's scent lingered in the air, he knew he was not the source of the anguish written on Max's face.

Max took some platters into the pantry and returned. He stared at Elliott. "Do you need something?"

Elliott gazed into Max's eyes. He hoped they might soften, but Max ceded nothing, glaring sternly at him.

"A brandy?" Elliott replied.

"Help yourself. I have too much to do."

"But Max!"

"Sorry."

"For what?"

"For sharing what I did. It's not your problem."

"It seems like destiny has something else to say about that," Elliott said, trying to figure out how he might bring up their encounter many years ago.

"I don't believe in that shit."

Elliott didn't believe in it either, at least not until now. But their coming together seemed uncanny. Elliott looked imploringly at Max, who evasively turned away from him to return spices to their spot on the shelf. Elliott didn't see the tears forming in Max's eyes.

Max waited for his emotions to quiet. He wiped his eyes and turned back to Elliott. All the fortitude he could muster wasn't enough to erase the desire he felt standing in front of Elliott. He briskly made his way past him. "I've got to take care of my chores."

Elliott grabbed his elbow. "Max."

"I can't," Max said, shaking Elliott's hands off his arm. He walked out into the dining room and began to organize chairs and tables.

Dumbfounded, Elliott decided Max's shame was intractable. He walked past him out into the parlor and the lobby, pausing at the desk to read the weather forecast posted on a card. "Wow!" he said to himself as he noticed that the extended forecast included heavy snow. "This isn't going to be good for skiing." With many of the slopes above the tree line, the stormy weather would create white-out conditions.

He had already begun to consider the idea of shortening his trip. The tension with Max was unnerving, and the inn was too small and intimate to avoid him. Sofia was increasingly difficult to read. He worried she was either onto him or into him; neither scenario a good one. He said to himself, "I'm going to check out tomorrow. It's for the best."

He was about to head upstairs when Sofia appeared at the desk. "Good night, Mr. Williams."

"Sofia. You are just the person I wanted to see," Elliott said.

"Is everything okay?"

"Oh yes. Things are fine. I just noticed the weather is going to be bad for several days, perhaps for the rest of the week. I have some urgent matters to attend to back in England, so I am going to have to check out early."

"Oh, that's terrible news. I hope we were not a disappointment." She worried that perhaps she had gotten too personal with Elliott at breakfast and had frightened him off or that Max had conveyed his annoyance too strongly.

"Not at all. The inn is wonderful, the food is amazing, and your hospitality is warm and accommodating. It's just, I have to get back."

Elliott could see concern on Sofia's face and added, "Don't worry. I'll cover the cost of the days I booked. I know you can't get new bookings for the days I reserved."

"Max will be so disappointed you are leaving."

Elliott wasn't sure of that, but he said, "I'll say goodbye to him tomorrow morning."

"I'll let him know," Sofia replied.

"Well. Thanks for your understanding. Good night," Elliott said warmly.

"Good night, Mr. Williams."

19

Chapter Nineteen – Death in Venice

Mürren December 1918

Clive stuffed the last pieces of clothing into his duffle bag and leaned it against the wall next to the others. His comrades had already gone out to have a beer in celebration of their return home. He begged off, preferring solitude before his departure the next day.

He walked downstairs, carefully avoiding Hans' office and the terrace where he and other TB patients had taken in the sun. Slipping out of the front door onto the main road, already covered in fresh snow, Clive walked toward the edge of town to make one last promenade along his favorite path with breathtaking views of the surrounding alpine landscape.

He passed Hans' and Margrit's house. Smoke rose from the chimney, and curtains were pulled back in the front windows. Clive glanced up and, to his surprise, Margrit was staring out of the window. Startled, she stepped back out of view. A moment later, she returned, wiped frost off the windowpane, and smiled at Clive, waving to him.

Clive waved back. Continuing forward, he heard a knocking on the glass. He glanced up over his shoulder and noticed Margrit waving for him to come to the house. He gave her a curious look and furrowed his brow.

She waved enthusiastically at him to come in. She stepped away from the window and suddenly appeared at the front door. "Clive! Clive!" she yelled.

He turned and walked toward her.

"Margrit. How are you?"

She didn't reply. She shook her head, apparently choked with emotion. "You going home?"

Clive nodded.

"No goodbye?"

Clive furrowed his brow, cognizant that he was remiss in not taking the time to say goodbye to her. Over the months, he had been invited to their home several times. They had grown close, sharing meals and spending long evenings discussing politics, the war, and literature. He and Margrit shared an understanding, an unspoken respect and concern for Hans, who seemed increasingly irritable.

"Hans said you are expecting a new baby?" Clive said, rubbing his hand over his belly to make sure she understood what he had said in English.

She nodded excitedly, warmly, but then quickly resumed her worried look.

"*Was ist los?*" Clive asked her what was wrong.

"*Es ist Hans.*"

"What's wrong with Hans?" he asked.

She continued to shake her head. "Some tea?" she offered.

Clive nodded and walked inside the house. He followed her into the kitchen, glancing around the apartment, fully expecting to see Hans.

"Conrad sleep," she said. "*Und Hans arbeitet.*"

Clive sighed, relieved he wouldn't bump into Hans, who was at work.

She heated water on the stove and placed some tea in a strainer. Soon the kettle whistled, and she poured water over the tea into the cup. She handed it to Clive, who breathed in the pleasant aromas and took a sip.

They sat at the kitchen table.

"I worry Hans," she said.

Clive gave her a quizzical look.

"*Er ist traurig.*"

Clive knew why he was sad, but he wasn't sure how much Margrit knew. "Is he worried about the new hotel?"

She shook her head no. "*Du.*"

"Me?"

She nodded yes. "Sad you leave."

"*Ich auch.* Me, too."

"*Bleib.* Stay."

"I can't," Clive said sorrowfully. He took another sip of tea.

"He love you," Margrit said without hesitation, without ambiguity.

Clive widened his eyes.

She nodded yes.

"*Ich liebe euch beide.*"

She nodded and smiled warmly. She knew Clive loved her, and she knew he loved Hans. She sensed Clive was avoiding the obvious, the special love and affection he had for Hans.

"*Eine besondere Liebe,*" she said in a low voice, one full of tenderness.

Clive didn't know how to respond. Yes, he and Hans shared a special love, and it seemed Margrit was more aware than he gave her credit for. But he could see the sadness in her eyes and said, "But you and Conrad? He loves you."

She returned a sullen and apathetic regard and an almost imperceptible nod no.

"He doesn't love me – not like he loves you and Conrad," Clive added emphatically, still nursing wounds from Hans' inability to declare his affection.

She nodded yes, implying that Hans loved Clive.

"No," Clive insisted.

Margrit cleared her throat in preparation for something she wanted to get off her chest. "*Auf Deutsch?*"

Clive nodded, hoping he could make out much of what she wanted to tell him.

In German, Margrit began, "Hans is a wonderful man. He is handsome, thoughtful, and responsible. We have a good life and a good home. But he is not happy."

Margrit's words didn't surprise Clive.

"When he talks about you, his eyes light up and he smiles."

Clive felt terrible for Margrit, wondering what it was like to be stuck with a man who didn't love her. He at least had the freedom to walk away. She couldn't.

Margrit tensed up. She appeared to want to ask something, to share something, but she either didn't know how to put it into words or was afraid to. "Sex?"

Clive lifted the cup of tea in front of his face to hide the sudden rush of blood to his cheeks. Margrit was trying to be honest with him, and he felt some compulsion to be honest back. He hesitated, and she added, "*Der Tod in Venedig. Thomas Mann.*"

Clive had heard of Mann's new book, a shocking story of an older man who becomes obsessed with a handsome youth in Venice only to succumb to an outbreak of cholera. It was full of allusions and metaphors, and it didn't surprise Clive that Margrit had read it, given what she had disclosed when they first met a year ago. She obviously suspected her husband was similarly inclined. It didn't seem to shock her, at least not anymore. She had made peace with it.

Clive knew that the main character in Mann's book was filled with shame and said, "*Er ist voller Scham.*"

Margrit wondered if Clive meant the character in Manns' book or Hans. In either case, it was true.

She nodded and asked, "*Mit dir auch?*"

"Yes. He feels shame with me, too," Clive said, avoiding any specifics, unnerved at how direct Margrit's line of questioning was.

She sighed, seemingly relieved that Hans didn't find her uniquely disgusting. "*Warum?*" she inquired, now curious about what appeared to be a more pervasive emotion in her husband.

"I don't know why," Clive replied. Margrit was beautiful. Clive could fully imagine being able to make love to her if he had to - if he had been married to her. Given what Hans had recounted, he imagined he felt shame for having sex with a man, not with a woman. Now he wondered if Hans felt shame around sex in general, with men and with women.

"*Er ist unglücklich,*" she observed.

As Margrit noted Hans' unhappiness, Clive had an epiphany. He wondered if Hans really wanted to be happy or even could be happy. The only time he had seen him animated and passionate was when he told him he was buying the Arven hotel. But with Margrit and himself, it was as if he couldn't say what he wanted, couldn't embrace his desires. As long as his affection for them was out of his control - something that happened to him or something he was obligated to - he could blame his unhappiness on them. It wasn't his choice. Therefore, he couldn't ever be the cause of his own unhappiness.

Clive wondered if Hans had been abused as a boy or teenager. Perhaps the event or series of exchanges had been so psychologically painful that his emotions around sex were frozen. As an adult, he felt sexual desire and shared sexual intimacy, but inside he was a little boy who had learned to stuff his feelings deep inside. He couldn't let anyone in for fear they would see the ugliness he felt inside. He was profoundly unhappy because sex was associated with powerlessness and unexpressed anger.

Clive realized that whatever the source of Hans' trauma, he couldn't fix it. He had tried.

He said sadly, "*Es tut mir leid. Ich muss nach England zurück.*"

Margrit nodded. A tear ran down her cheek. "*Du musst dein Glück finden.*"

Clive wasn't sure he would find happiness, as Margrit suggested, but he would at least be the one responsible for whether he was happy or not. He finished his cup of tea and stood. He walked around the table and gave Margrit a warm and tender embrace. "Find happiness where you can. Take care of Hans. Make the hotel a warm place where people can enjoy Mürren, as I have. It will bring you joy, I'm sure."

Margit nodded, as if she understood.

They walked to the front door, and Clive gave her one more embrace. He walked down the steps and onto the snow-covered road.

The next day, Clive joined his fellow soldiers as they gathered at the simple station to take the train to Grütschalp and then the inclined train to Lauterbrunnen. Most were excited to return home, thumbing photos of sweethearts they left before the war. Clive glanced out of the window as the train creaked to a start and began to weave its way through a forest of fir trees clinging to the rocky edge of the plateau. Through a few openings in the forest, he peered at the Jungfrau, the massive peak just on the other side of the valley. He smiled, thinking about the treks he and his comrades had made on gentle snow fields stretching from there to Grindelwald. He wondered how his life might unfold and what adventures awaited him in England. One thing he knew – he would be back. Probably never to Mürren. It was too fraught with heartache and disappointment. But the mountains were magnificent and inspired him to soar in his imagination. They fed his soul, and his heart, and had become his home. He would return.

20

Chapter Twenty – Understanding

France Winter 1928

Clive and Marie were seated alone in a comfortable compartment on the train from Basel to Paris, en route to England. Tourists were returning from St. Moritz, where the first official winter Olympics had just taken place. Clive and Marie had gone to the games at the invitation of Arnold Lunn. On the way back from St. Moritz, they stopped in Mürren to visit Hans and Margrit. Clive was reading a newspaper with reports about the athletes, and Marie was reading a novel. The wintery landscape passed swiftly outside the window.

Clive looked up and gazed at Marie. She seemed so serene and regal. She was a beautiful woman with brunette hair, luminous skin, high cheekbones, and luscious lips. He felt fortunate to have met and married her.

She sensed Clive's regard and glanced up, smiling at him.

"So, what did you think?" he asked her.

Marie gazed out of the window evasively, formulating her thoughts carefully. She turned back toward him and said, "Margrit is delightful. She was so warm, attentive, and hospitable. Their inn is marvelous. I'm not sure I'm a candidate for skiing, but I loved the alpine setting and the chance to walk in the snow. It was a marvelous vacation. I'm glad we were able to get away."

"Did you miss Henry?"

"Of course. But I'm sure my mother has taken good care of him. It was good to get away. Just the two of us."

"What did you think of Hans?" Clive asked, realizing she had not mentioned him.

"Hmm," she began tentatively. "He's very accomplished. I can't believe he continues to practice medicine and run an inn. He seemed very busy, though. I wish I could have gotten to know him better."

Clive nodded. Hans had been evasively busy to the point that Margrit became apologetic about his absences. Hans would disappear, leaving Margrit to entertain. Clive got the impression Hans was avoiding him. He said with chagrin, "Well, he has a lot of help from Tommy."

"Hmm. Yes," Marie murmured. Something had been troubling her since they arrived in Mürren. Tommy seemed especially solicitous of them – making sure their room was perfect, that they had extra portions at dinner, and that Clive had all the right ski equipment. He had an uncanny resemblance to her husband – dark wavy hair, a tall, robust frame, dark brown eyes, and a playful smile. She caught Tommy glancing at her husband with a certain intensity. She fully expected Clive to respond similarly, but he didn't.

She cocked her head slightly to the side and said, "I thought his relationship with Hans and Margrit a bit unusual, even presumptuous."

"How so?"

"He is the manager. He works for them. But he seems very familiar, intimate, and close to them both. There were a few instances where he used the term 'we' in reference to the three of them – as if they were a unit."

"Well, they all work together."

"Hmm," Marie murmured. "The references didn't have anything to do with work." She glanced off into the distance as if trying to recall something and then continued. "He made several comments about food and wine, as if all three shared the same preferences. And it sounded as if they all retire for bed at the same time. He even mentioned their common dislike for a radio program broadcast from Bern. There were several other remarks he made that implied a familiarity that I found peculiar."

"I imagine that running an inn requires a strict schedule everyone follows," Clive said defensively about their common time to retire to bed. "And I imagine they have grown friendly over the years and share common interests and dislikes."

"Still, the way Tommy spoke and behaved seemed strange. I wasn't expecting it from someone who is an employee."

Clive didn't find it surprising. In fact, he found it disturbing. In retrospect, he recalled a few apologetic glances from Margrit, as if she knew he, Clive, would be dismayed. Clive always wanted to believe that Hans loved him, even if he couldn't declare it. He hoped that deep down, he had been the one who made Hans happy, the one who made his heart flutter. Although it didn't surprise him that Hans had found a replacement, the intimacy between Tommy and Hans was painful to watch.

During their brief visit, Clive hoped to have received a protracted gaze from Hans - a look, a glance, some sign of affection and desire. Hans was particularly evasive, clearly not wanting

Clive to see something. Clive, too, had noticed Tommy's intimacy with the Webers, an intimacy that could have been his. He wondered if he had made a mistake in leaving ten years earlier. Perhaps Hans had come around, declared his love for Tommy, and garnered Margrit's understanding and acceptance.

Clive's eyes began to water. A tear streaked down his cheek.

Marie put her hand on Clive's knee and said, "Oh, dear. What's the matter?"

She knew the matter, but not the particulars. Her husband had been restless at the inn. At first, she chalked it up as a painful recollection of his internment and the conflicting feelings he must have had returning to a place that was so beautiful yet fraught with memories of the war. She detected a tension between her husband and Hans, but she assumed that it stemmed from Hans' personality; someone who had many obligations and a difficult time relaxing and enjoying his guests.

Marie caught Margrit looking affectionately at Clive several times when they first arrived. She wondered if there had been some kind of understanding between them, a romance or affair that took place when Clive was a prisoner. It caught her by surprise, since she always worried more about Clive's affection for men, not women. Clive didn't talk much about the war or his time in Mürren, so she was curious and eager to make sense of what was undoubtedly a pivotal moment in his life.

While Clive was friendly, even playful with Margrit, he was fixated on Hans. There were several remarkable instances when Tommy or Margrit were telling a story. Everyone was paying close attention, except Clive. He was either off in another world or staring at Hans, who was oblivious to Clive's regard.

Marie observed Hans' evasive demeanor toward Clive. Over the course of their stay, a quiet but palpable tension grew between

Hans and Clive. One evening at dinner, Tommy excused himself to take care of an emergency in one of the guest rooms. A few moments later, Hans excused himself to see if Tommy needed help. Margrit cast a glare at her husband, and Clive's whole body twitched. It was at that moment that Marie knew.

Clive's tears turned into sobs. He leaned toward Marie and rested his head on her lap. She stroked his hair. He murmured, "I'm sorry."

"There's nothing to be sorry about," she assured him. "I've always sensed you were carrying a heavy burden. It's time to let it go. Tell me."

Clive composed himself and pondered what to share with Marie. He loved her, and he loved their son. But the affection that had settled into the deepest parts of his heart had eluded him and now, he realized, was no more. He had hoped that Hans would have suffered as he had; that he would have grown weary of their separation and concluded that he should have told Clive he loved him. Clive would have accepted an apology or a belated statement of affection, but there was nothing.

Instead, Hans seemed happy. Tommy had replaced Clive and had become part of a curious *ménage à trois*. It should have been him.

Marie took the information in stride. Nothing Clive recounted surprised her. In fact, it helped her make sense of her husband's moods. Clive was loving and devoted, but his heart was elsewhere. She knew he loved her, but only to a certain point. It was enough for her, but she realized it was not enough for him.

"I can't believe the pain you have carried for so long," Marie assured Clive after he finished disclosing his past.

Clive gave her an incredulous look. He fully expected her to be indignant, embarrassed, and disgusted. Instead, she was tender and solicitous.

Marie cleared her throat and continued, saying, "I love you. But you need to be happy."

"I am," he protested.

She shook her head no. "Not really."

"I really am. I'm so fortunate to have you and Henry."

"But you need more."

Clive didn't respond, nor did his face betray any emotion. He knew she was right, but he found it difficult to admit his needs or imagine their satisfaction.

Marie caressed the side of Clive's forehead. She looked him in the eye and said, "I think you need to go back to Switzerland. It's a special place for you, one where you can be yourself. Why not go on a ski vacation each year – perhaps not to Mürren but to the towns nearby – Grindelwald and Wengen?"

"But," he objected.

She held her fingers up to his lips. "I insist. I can stay in England with Henry, and you can meet friends and express other facets of your life. I don't want to be a barrier to your happiness."

Clive's heart melted at Marie's tenderness and understanding. Choked with emotion, Clive found it difficult to say anything. He just nodded.

She then raised her hand and pointed her finger at him, saying, "But don't make a fool of yourself. You don't need to be someone's pet who grovels for scraps. You are smart, charming, handsome, and a catch. Don't sell yourself short."

"What about you?" he asked, wondering what Marie envisioned for herself.

She rested her chin on the back of her hand in thought. She paused, then said, "I haven't thought this through, and a lot of it depends on you. I want us to be a happy family and to have a good life. If you aren't happy, it drags us all down. You are my best friend, and I never want to lose that."

Wiping a tear from his eye, Clive said, "I assure you of my undying devotion and love."

"That means the world to me."

"I'm sorry to have put you through the weekend there."

"I'm sorry for you. It must have been very painful," Marie said tenderly.

"You can't imagine."

Marie and Clive returned home. Clive returned to Switzerland the following winter. He did so each winter except during the Second World War. He never returned to Mürren.

Over the years, he met men of his persuasion. Some were skiers; others worked at the hotel he went to each year. But he never got over his love for Hans.

He enjoyed the camaraderie of his friends, a tribe of men who discovered each other in a glance, a warm conversation with coded words, or a carefully placed hand on a shoulder or arm. He occasionally wondered what it would be like to have what he had with Marie with a man. And over the years, he met men who made his heart flutter and his legs grow weak. In each, there was a fragment of Hans – his haunting stare, the distinctive coloration of his skin, the solidity of his body, his tousled hair, his warm lips. When they expressed their affection, it was Hans he saw, Hans he heard, Hans he felt. The memory of Hans haunted him like a phantom, one he sought to hold and embrace. He longed to hear the words – I love you – but in each case, it wasn't Hans who voiced them, but an imposter, a stand-in.

Clive grew to treasure his companions, men who, like him, inhabited a parallel universe. It was home, a community of belonging. They all had similar stories and were forced to live in alien lands. But when they were together, they created beauty, magic, levity, and love. It was enough for him.

When Clive returned to England, his valises were full. He excitedly unpacked the joy and warmth he had brought home, sharing them with Marie and Henry. It was a good life.

21

Chapter Twenty-One – Auf Wiedersehen

ürren Winter 2007

Elliott didn't go to breakfast. He slipped downstairs earlier for coffee but returned to his room to pack. As predicted, the snow was falling heavily outside. He checked the schedule for trains and decided to catch one at 8:30 AM.

At 8:00, when he walked downstairs, he poked his head in the dining room to say goodbye. Sofia was busy with guests and looked up. She had a disquieting look on her face. She approached Elliott and said, "I suppose you are off."

"Hm hmm. I'm sorry for leaving early. And, again, everything was perfect."

But it wasn't, and Sofia knew it wasn't.

Elliott glanced around, hoping to spot Max. Sofia could tell Elliott was looking for him and said apologetically, "Max had to leave early this morning for some supplies. He said to give you his regards."

Elliott turned ashen. Max's decision to leave early was deliberate, and it stung.

Sofia noticed Elliott's consternation and distress. In all the years of their work together at the Traumblick, she had never seen Max react to a guest the way he reacted to Elliott.

"Tell him goodbye for me and give him this."

Sofia looked down at the envelope Elliott handed her.

"You can open it," he said, detecting her curiosity. "You've seen it already."

She opened the envelope. Inside was the postcard from Margrit to Clive, letting him know of Hans' death. "Oh, Elliott. This belongs to you."

"I want Max to have it. It belongs here – a memorial of Hans, Margrit, and the Traumblick."

Troubled, Sofia cleared her throat and said, "When I saw this the other day, I went into Hans' old files. I found your grandfather's chart."

Elliott's eyes widened. "Those still exist? From the first world war?"

Sofia nodded and continued hesitantly, "The notations in Clive's chart were odd. He had made a full recovery, as indicated in reports Hans made in March 1918. But just after the war ended in November, and plans were being made to send prisoners home, Hans noted that Clive's symptoms had returned and that he recommended a delay in his repatriation."

"Maybe Clive had a relapse."

"Suddenly, just before he was to go home?" Sofia said, furrowing her brow.

Elliott looked off into the distance, pondering Sofia's suggestion. "So, what do you think was going on?"

"If it was my guess, Clive and Hans had formed a bond. Hans didn't want Clive to leave and manipulated his chart accordingly."

"Are you sure? That's quite an unusual action for a physician to take," Elliott said, raising his brows.

"It is quite unusual, and so is the sudden change in the health status of a patient. That's why the only way it makes sense is if Hans didn't want Clive to leave."

"Could there be other reasons he didn't want him to leave?"

Sofia glanced off to the side and then turned back to face Elliott. "I've been struggling with this in my mind since I saw Hans' records and Margrit's postcard. The only alternative explanation is that Margrit and Clive had formed a bond, and Hans wanted Clive to stay for Margrit's sake. But that's really a stretch, as I think you say in English."

"Hmm. You're probably right."

"Your grandfather married, right?" Sofia asked thoughtfully.

"Hm hmm," Elliott murmured, deep in thought.

"Were he and your grandmother happy?"

"Seemingly," Elliott said hesitantly.

Sofia picked up on his hesitation and said, "But?"

"I remember friendship and respect, but I don't recall passion between them."

"It's an English thing, right?" Sofia chuckled.

Elliott grinned. "Yes, but my grandfather was very passionate when he came to the Alps. He had close friends – mostly men. He was playful, charming, and affectionate with them. Until now, it never made sense."

Sofia nodded, choked with emotion. A tear ran down Sofia's cheek. After what she had seen in the records, she imagined Hans had been desperate to keep Clive around. She felt like she was watching history repeat itself.

"You know, you made an impression on him," Sofia said suddenly, without context or prelude.

Elliott shook his head as if needing clarification. He wasn't sure if she was referring to Clive or Max.

"My brother has been struggling all these years. I've seen him carrying a heavy burden. I don't know what it is, but it has taken its toll. When he got back from the day skiing with you, I thought it had lifted."

Elliott shook his head quizzically. "Your brother? Max is your brother?"

"Yes. Didn't you know?"

"I thought you were married."

"Oh God, no! We're brother and sister. Neither of us has married. It's odd, although with Max it makes more sense."

"Hmm," Elliott said. "What do you mean?"

"Oh, it's just I think he's confused. Hasn't figured himself out yet."

Elliott nodded pensively, all sorts of questions now racing through his head. He glanced at his watch and realized he had to rush to the station.

Sofia noticed and reached toward Elliott, giving him a warm embrace. "Thanks for your understanding and sensitivity. I wish things had turned out differently."

"Me, too," Elliott said, realizing Sofia was probably an ally.

Elliott walked toward the front door. He bundled himself up and headed outside. Wind driven snow hit his face as he made his way up the hill into town. Few people were out. Some kids had sleds and were heading toward a hill.

With several startling revelations, Elliott wondered if his decision to leave was the right one. Before, he hadn't wanted to come between Max and Sofia, even if Max could come to terms with the deep wounds he carried inside. Hesitating as he walked up the hill to the center of town, Elliott almost turned back, but continued forward. He realized Max was unattached, but he seemed hopelessly bound by the trauma of the abuse he had endured. Elliott had spent a lot of time working on his own internalized homophobia, erasing the discomfort he felt when men looked at him with disdain, as if they had uncovered his secret craving. It was ironic that Max had contributed to Elliott's disquiet many years ago. It was all too weird and messy. He didn't want to take on Max's issues. Best move on, he resolved as he continued the trek toward the station.

The station was quiet and ghost-like. A few intrepid souls climbed into the carriages, like phantoms in a haunted tale. Elliott stepped inside an empty car, placed his luggage and skis near the door, and took a seat. He glanced out of the window into the angry weather raging outside.

At 8:30, a whistle blew, and the train creaked forward, making its way along the edge of the bluff. The train rocked back and forth as gusts of wind blew through the trees and hit the side of the carriages. Elliott wondered if the weather was trying to get his attention, dissuade him from his escape, halt his journey forward.

At Grütschalp, the conductor of the cable car advised passengers that the trip to Lauterbrunnen might not be possible, given the weather. Elliott wondered if it was a sign to go back, despite his reluctance to believe in such notions. The small group of travelers waited and eventually were advised that the wind had slowed just enough to permit them to continue. Elliott and others stepped inside the car. Soon they were floating in the whiteness toward Lauterbrunnen. Elliott detected a subtle odor in the air, one resembling his grandfather's cologne. He furrowed his brows, wondering what that meant.

Once on the valley floor, Elliott made his way to the train station. He continued to smell the scent of his grandfather's cologne. Dragging his suitcase and skis behind him, he made his way to the platform where the train to Interlaken would soon arrive. He realized he and Clive had passed through the same station several times before, and soon realized that the subtle hint of cologne floating in the cold air was Clive's. Elliott felt a chill fill his body. He was certain Clive was standing next to him.

He stood on the track and imagined Clive waiting for a train after the war. Given what he had learned, he had a new affinity for his grandfather, a bond they shared around their love of men, perhaps their love for Weber men. He imagined the anguish Clive must have felt as he left for England with a heavy heart. He wondered if the circumstances weren't similar, if Clive hadn't left out of concern for Hans' and Margrit's marriage, or perhaps some other matter that he and Hans couldn't work out.

A heaviness filled Elliott's heart; one he imagined his grandfather carried all of his life. He wished he could let it go, but he didn't know how. Soon the train from Interlaken arrived. A few passengers disembarked while others stepped into the cars, placing their skis and luggage near the doors.

Elliott stood frozen in place, unable to step onto the train but not sure what else to do. He felt as if he was no longer in control of his body, as if it had a mind of its own. The conductor made one last sweep of the area and whistled that the train would depart. The conductor stepped into the foyer, leaned out of the door, and waved to the engineer to proceed.

Elliott remained immobile on the platform, snow quickly covering his head and shoulders. As the train disappeared from the station, a sign appeared in front of him, pointing to the Grütschalp

Bahn and Mürren. It couldn't have been any clearer. He needed to go back.

A half hour later, Elliott approached the Traumblick and walked inside. Sofia heard the bell on the door and came out of her office. When she saw Elliott, she held her hand to her mouth and said, "Oh my God!" Her eyes watered.

Elliott smiled. He knew she was delighted at his return. He said, "I trust my room hasn't been rented out yet. I have some unfinished business."

Sofia nodded her head no. She came around the reception counter and gave Elliott an enthusiastic hug. "I'm so glad you returned."

"I just couldn't leave. Something or someone was tugging at me."

Sofia winked at Elliott. She was delighted that her brother had finally stepped out of his comfort zone, and she hoped Elliott might help him complete the journey.

"I have an idea." She gestured for him to follow her upstairs to his room. She helped him get situated and said, "Max will be back in a while. I'll let him know there's something that needs to be fixed in your room before the new guests arrive. Of course, there are no new guests arriving. Is that okay?"

"He won't be upset?"

"I have a feeling he will be pleasantly surprised."

"Are you sure?"

"Certain. I have never seen him so conflicted as he was this morning."

Elliott unpacked and sat in the chair facing the swirling snowstorm outside. His heart pounded anxiously in anticipation of Max's arrival and the inevitable surprise. He wasn't convinced Max would be happy to see him, but the persistent scent of cologne convinced him that Clive longed for a different ending, and he was ready to give it a try.

An hour later, Elliott heard a key slip into the door, and Max walked in, carrying a box of tools. He set them down on a side table just inside the door and glanced around the room. He spotted Elliott seated in the chair, glancing in his direction, smiling.

Max's mouth opened, and his eyes widened. At first, he blushed, embarrassed that he had tried to dodge Elliott's departure. He said, "I thought you might have left already. I had to get some supplies in town."

"Bullshit!" Elliott replied. "You didn't have the balls to say good-bye."

Max turned red in the face. He pivoted and headed toward the door.

"Don't run away, not like you did before!" Elliott commanded him with a firm voice.

Max paused and turned, giving Elliott a quizzical look.

"1970. Grindelwald. We met."

Max shook his head incredulously.

"It was at the Ibex Club. Do you remember?"

Max stared at Elliott and thought back to his teenage years. They were not happy ones, and he had done what he could to repress the memories, both the good and bad. He shook his head no.

"It doesn't matter. Just don't leave."

Max turned and ran down the stairs and walked into the office, where Sofia was responding to booking requests. "You tricked me."

"I don't know what you're talking about," she said, winking at her brother.

"I thought Elliott checked out; that he would be on the train to Interlaken and Zurich for his return to England."

"He came back."

"So, you sent me to his room for what purpose?"

"Max, you seemed so happy the other day after you two went skiing. I've never seen you that way before. Something lifted – a dark cloud you've been under for a long time."

"Well, I'm back to my normal dark self," he said emphatically.

"That's not good. You need to let go of what's troubling you."

He stared at his sister. He hesitated and said, "I can't."

"You can't or you won't?"

Max strained to breathe. There was terror in his eyes.

"What is it, dear?"

He rubbed his forehead with his fingers and shook his head. He repeated, "I can't."

"Are you gay? If you are, that's okay. I love you, and I want you to be happy."

Max gave his sister a stern look. He said emotionally, "It's not that."

"Then what is it?"

Another voice from the doorway spoke. "It's something that's been eating away at him for years, and it needs to be released."

Sofia and Max both looked up, surprised to see Elliott leaning against the door. Sofia gave both Elliott and Max a curious look. Elliott looked at Max and Max looked at Sofia as if he might disclose something. She peered into his eyes with love and tenderness.

Max shook his head. He began to pace back and forth.

Elliott said tenderly, "Max, you can say it. You aren't responsible for what happened. You are a good person, a loving person, a handsome person. You can let it go by naming it. Let the words take the hurt and shame away."

Sofia looked anxious, not sure what was to follow.

Max squeezed his temples with his hands. His face was full of anguish. He tried to vocalize a few words, but nothing came out. Finally, slowly, he said, "You know our great uncle Niklaus?"

Sofia nodded.

Max remained solemn, his hand shaking nervously.

Elliott gazed at Max and nodded encouragingly.

"He did something," Max said.

She gazed at him and then turned to Elliott, who nodded again, hoping Max would continue.

"He," Max started tentatively, choked with emotion. "He abused me."

"Oh, Max," she exclaimed, approaching him and giving him a warm embrace. "I'm so sorry. How horrible. When?"

"A long time ago. When I was sixteen."

"And you've been holding it in all these years?"

Max nodded. He began to cry. He rubbed his eyes with his hands. He wanted to leave the room out of embarrassment and shame. Sofia was standing in the doorway, blocking the exit to the owners' suite, and Elliott was standing in the doorway leading to the reception area. Elliott walked toward Max and reached his arms around him.

At first, Max bristled, trying to deflect Elliott's arms. He didn't feel lovable. He trembled and shook. Elliott gave Max space. He made a second attempt to hug him. Max acquiesced. Elliott could feel him relax. He finally felt safe, secure, and loved. Elliott ran his hands up and down Max's back. He could feel Max's heart pound and his chest rise and fall as he sobbed.

Max laid his head down on Elliott's shoulder and wrapped his arms around Elliott.

Sofia's eyes watered.

Elliott ran his hand over Max's head, stroking his wavy hair. He glanced over and noticed Sofia nodding affirmatively at the change in her brother. She walked toward them and gave Max a kiss on his cheek and stroked his temple. "I'm so sorry you've been carrying that burden all these years. Why didn't you tell me or dad?"

"I couldn't. I was too embarrassed."

Sofia looked over at Elliott and then back at her brother. "I know you've already heard this from Elliott, but it wasn't your fault."

"It feels like it."

"You were only sixteen. Our great uncle took advantage of you. You were vulnerable."

"I should have stopped it. I wasn't strong enough."

Sofia glanced up at Elliott. She realized now why her brother had such an impenetrable shell around him. He was cordial and friendly, but never let anyone in. Elliott was the first person with whom he let down his guard. For the first time in her life, she realized how powerful the attraction between two people could be, melting the protective barriers people erect around themselves. She wondered, now, if she hadn't created her own barriers, not from her own trauma but perhaps because she felt it in her brother, an under-the-surface apprehension that was palpable and frightened her, too.

"You're quite strong. Amazingly so."

Sofia thought back to their grandfather, Conrad, to the hard veneer he always seemed to wear, particularly with guests. She remembered how their grandmother was the person who interacted with guests and Conrad remained behind the scenes, taking care of the building, and finances, and orders. As she glanced over at Elliott, she couldn't help being struck by the amazing confluence of things – his ending up at the Traumblick, the relationship between his grandfather and Hans, and now the relationship between her brother and him. The universe seemed eager to fix something that was terribly amiss. She wondered if there wasn't a long line of sexual trauma or shame coursing through her family. She smiled warmly at her brother in Elliott's arms. It appeared that the cycle might be coming to an end. She sighed contently.

"I have an idea, Max. Why don't you and Elliott visit, spend some time together? I can handle the chores."

Max lifted his head and wiped a tear out of his eye. He looked into Elliott's eyes. They were dark yet full of tenderness. He had an odd sensation, as if he had peered into them before. The prospect of opening himself to another person, particularly to another man, still carried a lot of anxiety. He shook his head no, as if needing personal space. He said, "I think I need some time alone."

"No, dear. You need to talk things out with someone."

He shook his head again. He said emphatically, "Don't push me."

Elliott interjected, "Take your time, but I'm not going to leave. Your reaction years ago frightened me. But it doesn't anymore."

Max gave Elliott a quizzical look.

"Thirty-seven years ago, we met at the Ibex in Grindelwald. I made a friendly gesture that must have frightened you, given what you had just gone through with your great uncle. I still see the playful, sensitive, and handsome man that I met years ago. I don't want to walk away."

Max wanted to say, "I don't want you to walk away either," but it was too bold a declaration for him. Instead, he took Elliott's hand and said, "Mr. Williams. I think you said you needed something fixed in your room."

Elliott raised his brows and glanced over at Sofia, who nodded and smiled.

"Well, I guess I could stay a little while longer. The weather is frightful, and I have a stack of books to read."

"I hear you are an architect. Maybe we could engage your services to make some repairs to the inn."

"I don't come cheaply."

"That was obvious when you arrived with your starched shirt, alpine sweater, smug look, and expensive skis. We'll have to get you to relax a bit. We're a laid-back kind of place."

"You could have surprised me."

"Well, some guests put us on guard."

"The two of you!" Sofia remarked. "If you don't go upstairs right away, I'll put you to work."

Max glared at her. He squeezed Elliott's hand and said, "Let's go. She's serious." Max led them upstairs.

Sofia followed them with her eyes. As they rounded the corner, she overheard her brother ask, "So, we met at the Ibex?"

"Yes. And you suggested we might run into each other on the slopes."

"I did?"

"Yep. I just didn't realize how long it would take."

The End

Author

Michael Hartwig is a Boston- and Provincetown-based author. He is also an accomplished professor of religion and ethics as well as an established artist (oil painting).

Hartwig grew up in Dallas but spread his wings early on – living in Rome for five years, moving to New England on his return, and then working in the area of educational travel to the Middle East and Europe.

Hartwig imagines rich characters who are at crossroads in their lives. In many instances, these crossroads mirror cultural ones. There's plenty of sexual tension to keep readers on the edge of their seats, but the stories are enriched by broader considerations – historical, cultural, and philosophical.

Follow him on Facebook, Instagram, Goodreads, and Amazon Books.

For More Information Visit: www.michaelhartwigauthor.com

Other works include:

Crossing Borders
Old Vines
Entwined
First Crush
Oliver and Henry
A Roman Spell
Love Unearthed
Our Roman Pasts
A Collision in Quebec
A Man By The Pool
Transito Seville